DRAGON OF GLASS

ELVA BIRCH
ZOE CHANT

Dragon of Glass

© 2019 Zoe Chant and Elva Birch
All rights reserved

FAE SHIFTER KNIGHTS

Jingle bells and magic spells!

Fae Shifter Knights is a sizzling portal fantasy paranormal romance series with side-splitting humor, thrilling adventure, and heart. Each stand-alone novel features noble shifter heroes, brave and resourceful heroines who are fated to be their keys to magic in our world, adorable pets, and one bad-tempered, non-binary fae.

This book does stand alone, with a full character arc and a satisfying happy ever after, but it is part of a complete four-book series that will be most enjoyed in order:

>Dragon of Glass (book 1)
>Unicorn of Glass (book 2)
>Gryphon of Glass (book 3)
>Firebird of Glass (book 4)

CHAPTER 1

"Thanks for coming in on such short notice," Ansel said, as Daniella stomped the slush off her feet on the mat. "You probably have better things to do on the morning of Christmas Eve."

Daniella smiled. "I really appreciate the job," she said sincerely, unwrapping her scarf and unzipping her coat. "The extra paycheck will be nice when the Christmas bills come in."

Ansel pointed out the coat rack behind the sales counter and Daniella wriggled out of her jacket and hung it up with her scarf. She looked around the warehouse curiously.

She'd been to the old location of the second hand shop plenty of times, but Ansel had inherited the business several years ago and moved it a few blocks to the empty warehouse, re-branding it as an antique shop and attempting to get bargain-shopping tourists in; Daniella hadn't been in the new location yet.

It was a tall, echoing building with no windows at all. Rows of industrial shelving held tidy stacks of used merchandise: clothing, dishes, toys, and centuries of knick knacks. There were sections of ancient farm machinery towards the back that gave the place a slight scent of old oil, and clusters of antique furniture: dressers and chests and couches spanning decades of styles. There were smaller shelves crowded with books and CDs, and even VHS tapes and cassettes.

"I would have waited until after the holidays," Ansel explained, "but I wanted inventory done by year's end, and I'm leaving tonight. I won't be back until New Year's Eve, so you can just come in whenever you have time between now and then to get it done. The shop will be closed, so you don't have to worry about customers."

"That sounds great," Daniella said gratefully. "I've got hours scheduled at the cafe to work around, but I should have plenty of time to finish up next week."

Ansel himself was not what Daniella expected of an antique dealer; he was a young, brown-skinned man with short, tight curls dyed blond and he looked more like a jazz musician than a peddler of dusty furniture and vintage salt shakers. They knew each other in the way that you sort of knew everyone else in a small town; they'd seen each other at the grocery store, and maybe once at the cafe, but Daniella wasn't sure if they'd ever had a conversation until she found his post at the cafe cork board looking for a short-term assistant and called to apply.

He showed her the basic organization of the shop, and how the numbers should be entered in the ledger. It was old-school, just a grid-printed paper notebook. "You don't have to write out what each of these is," he pointed out. "I don't need to know how many Barbies or Strawberry Shortcakes there are, just broad categories like 'used toys.' Count out how many are on the one dollar shelf, how many are on the two dollar shelf, tally 'em up here."

They went briefly through the entire store, Ansel pointing out anything that was tricky. "Socks are by the pair, except the singles basket. Things sold in sets are one item altogether. It's all basically by price tag. If there's a sale price, use that; I sure don't plan to mark anything back up."

Daniella nodded as they walked back down one of the aisles. Ansel stopped to pick up a tag that was loose on the floor. "This is always a problem," he said. "People think they can tear off the tag and then dicker on the price. *Hey, if it doesn't have a price tag it's free, right?* As if I haven't heard that a thousand times this week." He glanced around, trying to see if it had fallen off something obvious. "If you do find something without a tag, either make a guess based on what's around it, or put it at the counter for me to figure out. The only really valuable stuff is up front under the counters, I promise you aren't going to accidentally sell a priceless vase for a buck."

But Daniella's attention had already been arrested by something beyond him on that aisle. There was a shelf dedicated to Christmas, with re-packaged tinsel and strings of neatly coiled lights—the old kind from before LEDs. It had holiday dish towels, pajamas, and three sizes of Santa hats. Above, hooks were screwed up into the underside of the next shelf, holding up a dazzling array of ornaments.

Most of them were cheap plastic things, out-of-the-box Hallmark collectibles, or glass balls in all colors. A few were handmade, made of wood or brass. Some of them looked like children's crafts.

But the one that caught Daniella's eye was near the back: a green, blown glass dragon with outspread wings. It was hanging in a ring of white glass, but looked like it would sit freestanding as well if it were unhooked from the gleaming circle. It shifted in an imperceptible breeze in the warehouse, and glimmered in the dim lighting. "Oh," Daniella murmured. "Oh..."

"... worry about the difference in quality." Daniella realized that Ansel had been talking to her.

"I'm sorry, what?" She was embarrassed; she was usually much better at focusing, especially on the first day of a new job.

Fortunately, Ansel looked amused. "There's a lot of interesting junk here. Not even sure where most of it came from."

"I've been keeping an eye out for a Christmas ornament," Daniella admitted, knowing that he'd caught her distraction. "My parents took all the ornaments when they moved to Florida and I'm just starting my own collection."

"I've definitely got some one-of-a-kind pieces," Ansel chuckled, fingering a sled made from Popsicle sticks and pipe cleaners.

"How much is the dragon?" Daniella asked impulsively. "I've never seen anything like it."

"Oh, that glass one? I'm surprised it's still in one piece. It used to be part of a set, but I'm not sure what happened to the rest of them. It's handmade, does it have a tag?"

Daniella reached carefully between the ornaments and lifted the dragon off the hook by its hanger. It was heavier than it looked. "Twenty," she breathed, as the tag rotated into view.

"You've got a ten percent employee discount..." Ansel said, but whatever else he might have said vanished as Daniella let the ornament rest carefully in her hand.

With the cool touch of the glass, she was suddenly on fire.

Heat rushed through her chest, blooming in her breasts, and Daniella felt her loins suddenly awaken. Her ears and cheeks blazed and her knees went weak. She was grateful for the dim lighting in the warehouse and the slight natural tan to her skin that should hide the worst of her abrupt blush.

It was everything she could do to stay on her feet as a wave of pleasure washed over her.

"I'll get it," she squeaked, before she realized that Ansel had already moved on down the aisle and was pointing out another kind of special tag.

He nodded casually, like she hadn't just had a world-crumbling experience, and Daniella tried to smile brightly in return.

She could breathe again if she stopped touching the glass, and she took the rest of her orientation awkwardly holding the ornament by the hook.

Fortunately, there wasn't much more to see. They went back to the counter, where Ansel showed her where the bags and packing material were and wrapped the dragon and its ring carefully in tissue and bubble wrap and put it in a bag.

"I'm sorry," Daniella said, feeling uncomfortable and flustered as she handed him cash. "I'm not usually so impulsive, I just… I'd been looking for one… and…" she trailed off. What was she supposed to say? *And this one just gave me the best orgasm of my life?*

Ansel shrugged and Daniella hoped that she hadn't just bombed her job opportunity. But Ansel seemed pretty easy going, and he gave her a key without hesitating. "It sticks a little, so you might have to give it a good wiggle."

Wiggling was the last thing Daniella wanted to think about at the moment.

"Thanks," she said brightly. "I appreciate the job." She did, too. It was a big project, but she thought she could get it done in the time he'd asked, and Ansel was offering pretty generous pay for a small town with few opportunities. She tucked the bag into her over-sized purse.

"So, ah, I'll probably get started the day after tomorrow," she said, as Ansel showed her where the light switches were and started to shut them down.

"Right," he agreed. "I honestly don't expect you to work on Christmas like some kind of Scrooge."

Daniella giggled nervously and they left the warehouse. She used her key to lock it, keenly aware of Ansel's scrutiny. It did require some wiggling.

"Merry Christmas," they said together, then Daniella headed down the sidewalk towards her car, hyperconscious of the fragile burden in her purse. She was definitely going to need to change her underwear before she went to work.

CHAPTER 2

Trey was floating.

No, floating implied some sort of grace. Trey was *floundering*.

Knights do not flounder, he told himself firmly, but his best intentions seemed to have no effect on his situation; he was still definitely not in control of his limbs.

He did not, in fact, seem to *have* limbs.

If floundering was a failure of dignity, being a disembodied awareness was decidedly worse.

Wasn't he in the midst of a battle? Memory began to flood back. He had been losing a battle, which simply would not serve. Robin had been shouting, Henrik… Henrik had been trying to cast a counterspell.

Trey tried to shake a head that didn't exist, with no more success than moving his limbs.

He wasn't alone, but he didn't recognize any of his shieldmates. This was a new presence in his head.

Fear flashed through him. Was he being taken over? Was this the act of a dour?

As fast as the fear was, faster still was the feeling that

followed it—intense, bright sexual desire, a wave of it so keen it almost hurt, and Trey was left with a feeling of longing and need.

The presence was gone, and Trey had never felt so alone.

~

"I'm sorry, Fabio, I'm so sorry!" Daniella juggled her bags to one arm so she could dig into her purse. She had just dropped her keys into it, how could they possibly be at the bottom already?

On the other side of the door, Fabio was whining pitifully and Daniella could hear his nails scrabble at the sill. "No digging!" she scolded. "I'm coming, sweetie! I had to get groceries with the entire population of town apparently. I know you've been patient..." She found the keys at last and wrenched the lock open.

Fabio paused to head butt her in panting, happy greeting, then streaked past her for the side yard, his silky fur rippling in the afternoon light. As an Afghan Hound, it was a lot of silky fur, and he looked like more like a Muppet than a supermodel.

Daniella squeezed into the house with her bags and switched on the light with her elbow, grinning at the sight. She'd splurged for a real tree that year, in all its needle-shedding glory, and the room was filled with the delicious smell of pine. There was barely room to squeeze past it to the couch, but it was twisted with colored lights and ropes of tinsel. There were no ornaments on it... yet. She still had the bag from the second hand store tucked carefully into her purse.

She dropped the other bags onto the kitchen counter and slung her purse over the chair, then started dutifully unpacking the groceries. With absolutely no self control, she had splurged on everything Christmas. Eggnog, one of the fancy spiral smoked hams, and ugly orange yams that she hoped she could figure out how to cook with a package of mini marshmallows. A pumpkin pie, a jar of fancy black olives, and a bulk bag of chestnuts that Daniella had a vague notion she could roast in the oven. She'd even bought a tiny fruitcake, figuring that it couldn't possibly be as terrible as she remembered.

It was too much food, she realized with chagrin as she packed it into the crowded fridge. She'd bought enough food for a family, not a single girl and her dog. Well, it was her first Christmas on her own, and it wasn't like you could buy less than a whole pumpkin pie.

Daniella went back to the door. "Fabio! Come on, boy! I'm sure you've done what you needed to by now."

Fabio came rushing eagerly back and tried to jump up and lick her face. "I missed you too," Daniella said, kneeling to ruffle behind his silky ears. "Oh my gosh, you need a good brushing, you mangy mutt."

Fabio, confident that she was giving him the greatest of well-deserved compliments, danced in a circle and returned to lick her face again.

"Come on, you fabulous flirt, I'm not going to have time to give you a w-a-l-k yet. I get to shower and go to my regular job." Daniella stood back up and brushed off the knees of her jeans. Fabio edged past the tree that he still hadn't entirely made peace with and jumped up on the couch to watch her soulfully over the cushions.

"Wait until you see what I found today!" Daniella dug into her key-eating purse and carefully pulled out the bubble-wrapped package. "Our first ornament!"

Daniella hadn't wanted to start her own Christmas traditions with a tacky box of plastic balls made in a factory overseas. She wanted to curate something special, something personal, with every ornament holding a memory.

She unwrapped the ornament on the kitchen table, careful not to actually touch it this time. She was grateful to see that all the fragile bits of glass were still in place as she peeled back the layers of tissue. Fabio tried to nose it and she scolded him. "Back, Fabio." She picked it up by the hook, and, unable to resist, touched it gingerly with her fingertips.

The knee-weakening sensation was exactly as she remembered, but this time there was more.

She was very suddenly someplace else, floating in nothingness filled with light... and she wasn't alone.

There was a dragon before her, a great, glossy green dragon with wings spread out in surprise. It was like the ornament, and yet not; it had the same graceful curve to the neck, and the same elegance, but this was a living, breathing thing, with great, dark eyes and wicked claws.

Have you come to free me?

Its voice—*his* voice—was deep and smooth and disturbingly sexy. Or maybe it was just that Daniella was still completely keyed up from earlier.

Ah... she said, feeling stupid and slow. *How would I do that?*

Are you a witch? the dragon asked.

While Daniella was wondering how to answer that, there was a sudden jolt and she was standing in her little house again, Fabio licking her hand dangerously close to the fragile ornament she was holding.

"Woah!" she said, pulling it up out of his reach.

A dragon.

There was a dragon with a crazy-sexy voice trapped in her Christmas ornament.

Daniella made herself shut her eyes and shake her head.

Fabio whined at her.

"I know," Daniella said. "I know, I'm nuts. You've just witnessed your dog-mom losing her ever-loving mind." She put the ornament down on the table hard enough to make her wince. It was all she could do not to pick it up and inspect it for damage. She didn't touch it again.

But it was just a Christmas ornament. Eighteen dollars at the second hand store had probably been highway robbery for it.

She backed away. She would just take a shower, and when she was done, it would still be just a pretty piece of green silicone dioxide on her kitchen table, but it wouldn't be making her hallucinate or get hot.

As the water for the shower ran warm, Daniella convinced herself that she had just had a waking dream. The voice she'd heard was just a quiet little moment of imaginary nonsense caused by working double shifts at the cafe and reading too many books. The dragon... she hadn't seen a dragon. That was absurd.

It had been such a *sexy* voice.

That was all it was, she decided, stepping into the tub and letting the hot water cascade over her. She'd had a runaway fantasy, born of too much loneliness and devouring too many romances. She'd found something shiny and fixated all of her desires on it because she was tired and not being sensible.

But if there was one thing that Daniella was, it was sensible. So she was going to shower efficiently and get dressed for work at the cafe, and she wasn't going to think about the dragon ornament.

She wasn't going to think about how touching the ornament had made her feel and she wasn't going to imagine what kind of sexy body might come with that sexy voice, and she certainly wasn't going to fantasize about that while she was in the shower soaping off her very naked body.

She tripped over Fabio coming out of the bathroom, despite the fact that he was always there when she came out, whether she'd been there an hour or just thirty seconds.

"You could not be more in the way if you tried," she told him, like she did every time.

He groaned and rolled over so she would pet his belly with her bare foot.

Daniella dressed in her cafe uniform, but left the shoes off her already-aching feet. At least the last shift on Christmas Eve ought to be pretty slow and people should tip well in the holiday spirit.

As she came out of the bedroom, she caught sight of the ornament on the kitchen table. It cast verdant light across the cheap marble laminate.

She was sensible, she reminded herself.

She didn't believe in magic, or witches, or *dragons*. It was just a shiny glass sculpture. She was going to make herself a sandwich and go *sensibly* to work.

But first, she was going to hang up her new very-definitely-not-magic Christmas ornament on her very-definitely-not-magic tree.

She cautiously picked up the ornament by the silvery hook. It was just a heavy piece of green glass. She lifted it high and let it catch the light.

Just an ornament.

Have you come to free me?

Daniella loved fairy tales. The idea of breaking an evil enchantment was so beautiful. And she knew that spells were often broken with kisses.

If it was just an ornament, it wouldn't hurt anything to give it just a little kiss.

And if it broke the spell...

Daniella brought it up to her mouth, aware of Fabio watching her curiously, and gave it a brief, embarrassed kiss.

She closed her eyes, because that was the sort of thing you did when you kissed something. And of course, with Fabio you always risked being licked on the eyeball.

The light that flashed against her eyelids was green and when Daniella opened her eyes in surprise she was momentarily blinded. Fabio began barking in frenzied alarm.

Daniella dropped the ornament that she was still holding...

… and it was caught by a long-haired man standing naked in her living room, crowded up against the back of the couch beside the tree. "Lady," he said, in a rusty voice.

Then, to her shock, to Fabio's delight, and to the Christmas tree's danger, he knelt at her feet, pressing the ornament to his very bare chest. "You have released me… alack!"

Any face at Fabio's level was fair game and he had gotten past his brief alarm bark to press forward and greet the stranger enthusiastically.

"Fabio, back!" Daniella wasn't sure who she was really worried for; the man had arms like barrels and had no trouble holding Fabio back, but her dog was a lot to take at face level. And there was a lot of skin being licked.

A lot of really gorgeous skin.

"I'm sorry," she gasped, reaching forward to grab Fabio's collar and trying desperately not to *look*. "He's just… really friendly."

CHAPTER 3

The mortal woman and her hound were understandably frightened by Trey's sudden appearance and he immediately moved to put them at ease. The hound was easily subdued with scratches and went into an ecstasy of wiggles and whines when Trey found the correct places for attention.

"Your hound is... er... an admirable protector, Lady," Trey said as the dog fell over onto the floor with his tail thumping wildly on the floor.

"He's a goon," the woman said, voice strangled. "I was... sort of expecting a dragon. I saw... there was... a dragon."

Trey looked up at her, taking in the strange clothing and the very odd decor. A witch, most likely. The dwelling was small but full of wondrous things, not the least of which was a tree growing in the center of the room which was somehow on colorful fire but not burning.

"I am a dragon," he said firmly. "Though..." he looked down. "Where is my armor? My sword?"

"That's a very good question," the woman agreed. She

was looking anywhere but at him; he had clearly offended her sense of modesty. "But a better question is who the hell are you and what are you doing in my living room?"

Trey raised the ornament that he still cradled in his hand. "I am Trey, dragon knight, protector of the realm, defender of the fallen crown. I cannot say for sure how I came to be here, but I suspect that I have been trapped in this." He frowned. "There was an ambush. My team and I were caught in a spell. I must locate my shieldmates and return to my battle!"

"Your team of dragon knights," the woman said flatly. "You were trapped in an ornament… by a magic spell."

"No, lady," Trey said apologetically. "We are not all dragons."

She looked at him skeptically. "Oh, of course not."

"Henrik is a griffin," Trey explained. "Rez is a unicorn. Tadra is a firebird. Our teacher, Robin, is a fable."

"Right." Her tone was dubious.

"I would shift, and show you, but I fear your cottage could not contain my true form. If you would like to go outside, I could…"

"Oh, no," the witch said hastily. "No, no, no. I mean, the neighbors would surely enjoy the show, but, no."

Trey stood and she drew in a hasty breath, staring fixedly away from him.

"I have some clothes that might… ah… fit you," she suggested breathlessly.

"It would be appropriate to be more attired than this," Trey agreed.

"Just… wait… here," she squeaked, starting to retreat into an inner room. "I'll be right back."

"Wait!"

She ran into a door frame and clung to it, turning back to accidentally look directly at him. "Mm?" she managed.

"Do you have a title I might properly address you with?" Witches could be tricky business and an inconsiderate slight might be the difference between her assistance and a troublesome curse.

"A title?" she said in surprise. "Um. Not really. My name is Daniella."

Trey let his breath hiss in; he hadn't expected the witch to give him her name. He bowed his head. "My thanks, Lady Daniella," he said sincerely. "I shall honor your trust."

After a moment of silence, Daniella cleared her throat. "Clothes. I was going to get you clothes. Hang on."

She disappeared into the inner chamber, leaving Trey alone with her guardian hound.

The hound looked up at him adoringly and thumped his tail on the floor more soundly.

A closer inspection of the tree revealed that it was actually hung in reflective metal, so fine and soft that it shimmered like silk. What he had assumed was fire proved to be a string hung with tiny glowing lanterns in a rainbow of hues. The colored light bounced from the silvery metal decorations.

A growling sound from a large white cabinet caught Trey's attention and he wondered if the witch had other animals under her thrall as he went to explore the other room. There was a water pump in a sink, but the lever to operate it looked small and insufficient. He gave it an experimental pump and was astonished when water began to pour from the faucet with no further effort. He quickly returned the pump handle to its original position and the stream ceased.

This was clearly a sorceress of some power. Numbers blinked in ominous glowing letters from a panel above a smooth surface cluttered with pots and pans of incredible quality. A small, flat clock was merrily keeping time on the wall, with no sign of weights or cranks.

Trey refrained from opening any doors or drawers, not sure what protections Daniella might have on her belongings and not willing to risk her ill will.

It was hard to imagine ill will from her, though. She had innocent brown eyes in a round face, and the waves of her mahogany brown hair were soft and loose. Her strange clothing did little to conceal the curves of her short, lush body; she was definitely no child.

But she wasn't the hardened hag that Trey would have expected of her profession, either, and he was alarmed by how appealing he found her. He knew better than to lust after a witch. He also had duties far more pressing than satisfying his baser desires.

The hound had followed him hopefully into the room that Trey was suspecting was a kitchen and was sitting near the entrance.

"Worthy hound," Trey addressed him. "May I please you with a treat?"

"Fabio," Daniella said from the doorway. Trey was equal parts alarmed that she had been able to approach without warning, and confused by her statement.

"Fabio?" It wasn't a word that he knew. Was it a spell?

"The hound. Er, my dog. His name is Fabio. I named him after the romance cover model, because of his fabulous hair."

Daniella was looking not at the hound, but at Trey's hair, loose over his shoulders.

Trey ought to have been afraid of her interest, because any attention from witches was risking damnation.

But he couldn't look at her and not wonder if his soul wouldn't be a small price for her affection.

She was breathtakingly lovely, with flushed cheeks and

plump lips. Her hair was enchantingly lustrous and full. It was a little damp, as if she had just come in from rain, though her clothing was dry.

Clothing. She was holding an armful of clothing, to Trey's gratitude. Her cottage was not an appropriate temperature for nudity and his continued thoughts about her beauty were beginning to have an unwelcome effect.

"You have garments?" he said in an adolescent voice, trying to decide if he should cover himself. He cleared his throat in embarrassment.

"Oh god, garments, yes. Please put garments on! Here!" She thrust them at him and turned violently away.

CHAPTER 4

It was almost a shame to put him in clothing, but if Daniella was expecting him to look ridiculous in her sweatpants and t-shirt, she was sorely disappointed.

Her baggiest sweats were taut around his legs and undoubtedly across his butt as well—Daniella was trying very hard not to look as she went to the kitchen to make sandwiches. She had waffled between a Led Zeppelin band t-shirt and a sparkle unicorn shirt that was a slight bit larger. Size considerations had won over dignity, but Trey had lost exactly none.

It took a lot of man to look macho in a girly glitter shirt, but Trey was clearly a *lot* of man. His arms were simply massive and Daniella had never wanted to stare at a unicorn as much as this one, stretched across his chest.

He hadn't even hesitated at the decoration on the shirt, only smiled at it in approval and smoothed it down over his sculpted pecs with apparent pride.

Now that he was wearing clothing over his very distracting body, she was more aware that it wasn't just his chiseled build that was making her knees feel weak. He was rather dazzlingly handsome on top of that, with perfectly beautiful, strong features and a head full of long blonde hair that gave Fabio—either the dog or the cover model—a run for their money. His eyes were utterly gorgeous: leaf green and soulful and sweet.

Daniella made herself stop staring.

"I'm not going to get to work with enough time to eat first," Daniella told him, marching herself into the kitchen to open a bag of bread. "You want a sandwich? Allergic to anything?"

Trey frowned at her. "A sandwich? Allergic?" He eyed her activity and said cautiously, "I would not be so discourteous as to refuse your hospitality..."

Daniella opened the fridge. "I have some ham and Swiss cheese, if that sounds good."

Trey, his eyes huge, looked around the door of the fridge in awe. "What is this wondrous thing?"

"Ham and Swiss?" Daniella asked, but Trey was cautiously putting a hand into the space. "Oh, you mean the fridge?"

"Fridge," he echoed. "It is... a portal to the cold outside?"

"A portal? No, it's a Maytag. Bottom of their brand, but it works great."

He looked like he wanted to touch a ketchup bottle in the door but hesitated. "It is... a storage device?"

"Yes," Daniella said, nodding slowly. "It preserves food."

Trey gave an admiring whistle. "Does it slow time?"

"What? No. It's... just cold." She took mustard and mayonnaise from the door and went to the counter, casting a look back at Trey, who was still gazing into it. "And I pay for that cold, so I'd appreciate it if you didn't leave it open forever."

He closed it swiftly at her hint and came to watch her assemble the sandwiches. "All magic comes with a price," he said sagely.

"It's not… you know what, it's magic. That's as good as anything else."

Daniella had read too many books not to have suspicions about where Trey had come from. Clearly there was something mystic afoot, though she still doubted Trey's claim to be a dragon, even after the hallucination from the ornament. Was he a time traveler? From some alternate dimension? Wherever he was from, they didn't have refrigerators, or apparently sandwiches, because he stared at the plate she offered him in wonder.

"It's food," Daniella assured him. "Delicious food."

She demonstrated by taking a bite.

She put her plate on the kitchen table and cleared off her second chair. "Sorry, I don't have company often."

"Are we very far from civilization?" Trey asked, politely sitting in the chair once Daniella had found a place to put her mail. He tasted the sandwich, smiled his approval, and proceeded to practically inhale the rest of it.

"It… ah, depends on how you define civilization," Daniella said, trying not to stare as he ate. He had a jaw like a Roman god. "We're a ways from a major city, but we're basically downtown Wimberlette."

"Wimberlette," Trey said thoughtfully. "I do not know that province. Has the fallen crown been restored to the throne?"

Daniella furrowed her brow at him. "Wimberlette is a town. A small town in Michigan, in the United States of America. I've never even heard of a fallen crown, but this is a democracy."

Trey didn't seemed stunned by the news. "I suspected I was not near my home," he said gravely.

"Or possibly your time," Daniella pointed out.

He looked her in the eyes and Daniella wanted to stay there forever. "Or possibly my time," he agreed sadly.

"So, can we get you back there?" Daniella had to ask, almost reluctantly. He was the most gorgeous thing she'd ever seen and he was polite and adorably clueless; part of her wanted to beg him to stay. Part of her... or parts of her. She kept fantasizing about kissing him, about what his arms would feel like around him, about what his hair might feel like falling over her... and remembering what it had felt like when she touched the glass ornament he'd been imprisoned in.

"I would be grateful for your assistance," Trey said softly, gazing at her longingly.

When Daniella's phone went off in her pocket, for a moment, she thought he'd given her heart palpitations set to imaginary music. "Oh," she said faintly as he stared at her in awe. "I have to get this."

It was Marie from the cafe. "Are you coming in?"

"Yes," Daniella assured her. "I was just running a little late, so I'm eating here. I'll be there in..." she looked at the clock. "Ten minutes.

"Okay," Marie said gratefully. "I just wanted to make sure I could let Leann go early. It's been slow."

"No problem, I'll see you in a few."

Daniella looked at Trey, who had lifted up his plate to lick the crumbs off. "I have to go to work," she said. "Are you... are you going to be okay here for about six hours?"

"Alone?" Trey asked, an absolute embodiment of Fabio's expression when he realized that Daniella was leaving him home and going out.

"Fabio will be here," Daniella said, finding her shoes under the table.

Fabio, hearing his name and noticing that she was

putting on shoes, materialized from nowhere to pant in excitement and get underfoot.

"You can watch TV," Daniella suggested desperately. "Oh, here, I'll show you how."

She found the remote in the couch cushions and turned on the television. A strident woman in a reality show was complaining about a fellow contestant. "Er, how about something else," she suggested, flipping channels. She rested briefly on the news, which was talking about crimes and strife, and flipped through to a channel showing non-stop holiday movies. "Here we go."

Trey stared.

"It's television, it will rot your brain if you watch too much," Daniella felt obligated to warn him. "Here's the remote. Power on, power off. Change channels, volume up and down."

Trey took it as if she had just handed him a magic wand. Daniella supposed that in some ways, she had. "Any technology, sufficiently advanced," she muttered. "I'm sorry. I have to leave, but I'll make dinner when I get back, and you can help yourself to anything." She glanced at her kitchen. "Let's say anything on the counters. Most of the rest involves cooking." There was an array of crackers and easy snacks. He'd be fine.

To her surprise and pleasure, he knelt at her feet. "You honor me, Lady Daniella."

"Just Daniella," she managed to squeak. "Just Daniella..."

Trey stood and he swept her hand up to his mouth as he did so. "Not just Daniella," he said intensely. "I don't understand much about what is happening, but I know I would not be here if I was not meant to be."

Daniella backed into the door frame that was right behind her.

"Oh, you don't have to... ah... that's... it's..." His mouth on her knuckles seemed to have short-circuited her brain functions. "I have to go. Fabio, stay. Oh, if you could walk him once, the leash is there, you know what, I don't think you should go out, just stay here. Watch Christmas movies. There's ice cream in the freezer."

Her hand was her own again and she had no idea what to do with it. "Thank you, er, Lord Trey."

"Just Trey."

"Trey," Daniella said breathlessly. Then she pulled on her coat, kneed Fabio out of the way so she could slip outside, and bolted down the walk to the front curb.

She walked swiftly down the sidewalk and with every step away from her house, it seemed more and more impossible that she'd just left a gorgeous man who was claiming to be a dragon knight wearing her sweatpants and watching her television.

CHAPTER 5

Trey attempted to have a conversation using the smooth rectangular portal that the witch—Daniella—had opened for him, but swiftly realized that it was intended only for observation.

He perched on the couch and was joined by Fabio. After a brief, eager investigation with his nose and tongue, the silky-haired dog curled up and fell asleep next to him.

The observation portal showed a play titled *It's a Wonderful Life* and Trey watched avidly as a man saw the effect of his own life once it was erased. Had his life been erased, when he'd come to this strange place? He was baffled most by strange interruptions in the story that were loud and garish compared to the play, expounding the value of eating establishments selling strange, colorful food, financial services, and an absurdly-dressed man talking about the finest used cars and trucks available at rock bottom prices.

When the play ended, another followed it, *A Christmas Story*, which appeared to be the antics of children hoping for inappropriate gifts (Trey still wasn't certain what a BB gun was besides a type of ranged weapon that was disapproved by parents and coveted by youths). Trey was too baffled by the story to enjoy it much.

The imagery then changed to an illustrative form of animated artwork. Trey was again enthralled by a simple story of a man named Charlie Brown selecting an unsuitable Christmas tree. He looked at Daniella's Christmas tree with new appreciation. His own glass ornament hung upon it, glinting against the colored lights.

"If you watch too much of that, it'll rot your brain," a familiar voice told him.

Trey spun, reaching automatically for a sword that wasn't at his side. "Robin! Master fable!"

Fabio, startled from sleep, stood and began to bark in alarm.

It took Trey a moment to recognize what had confused him about Robin's appearance. "You are *tiny*," he said in astonishment.

"I am *diminished*," the small form said, sounding insulted. Gone was the tall, winged figure that Trey was familiar with. Robin was still neutral in appearance, neither female or male, lithely built but strong. They had the same long mane of brown hair and dark eyes as always, and their wings were still transparently webbed over a dark patterned framework like a dragonfly... but they were barely two handspans high. They were wearing ill-fitting clothing in odd patterns and their feet were bare.

Fabio went from barking to whining and dancing around underneath Robin's winged form as if he thought it was a toy being held just out of reach.

"Can you tell me what has happened? Why are we here? Why are you...?" Trey chose not to finish the sentence. "Where are we?"

Robin dropped from the air where they'd been

hovering and alighted on the kitchen table, folding their wings behind them. Excited, Fabio dove for them but Trey caught him by the collar and held him back. Robin paced to the edge of the table and sat down, legs dangling. "I failed you."

"You could not," Trey said with more confidence than he felt. He still did not precisely understand how he had gotten here or what the outcome of their battle had been, but he trusted that it was not Robin's fault.

"I could not keep the dour-ridden from returning, and they came at the boots of many bleaks."

Trey felt a growl in his throat, but forced it down. Fabio had ceased to struggle against him and was trying, instead, to twist around and lick Trey.

"Their purpose?"

"You four," Robin said gravely. "They knew that you could stop them, that you were the only things that possibly could, and they came with spells I've never seen or imagined, planning to break you."

Trey looked down at his body. "I am unbroken. Did the spell fail?"

"The spell was successful," Robin said, pointing at the glass ornament on the tree. "But their attempt to break you afterwards was thwarted. Henrik cast a confusion before he was transformed and in the resultant muck, I was able to smuggle the four of you through a portal… here. To this world. I asked for someplace safe rather than something specific and this world is where it sent me."

Fabio took advantage of Trey's distraction and stepped forward to stick his narrow nose directly into Robin's stomach. Robin grunted and whispered a few words of power. Fabio retreated, shaking his head in confusion, and sat down obediently.

"What *is* this world?" Trey had to ask. It was *Daniella's* world in his mind.

"It is an innocent world," Robin said. "What our world might have been without dours, without bleaks."

"Without Cerad," Trey guessed, frowning.

"They have their own monsters, but all of them pale in comparison," Robin said. "I've been here a year, learning their ways. The leylines here are not tuned quite the same way as they were in our world and I cannot tap as much magic. That is why..." they gestured at their small form. It was hard to take Robin seriously in this smaller size; they were like a child's doll.

"Can you return us to our world?" Trey asked. "We must go back and protect the kingdom..."

"It's been a year, and you missed that part where the kingdom already fell," Robin said shortly. "Its heroes are gone. It doesn't exist anymore. Not like you knew it. The dours are everywhere. Everyone who lives is ridden."

Trey sank into the kitchen chair, releasing Fabio. "You tried to go back."

"I tried," Robin said, their head bowed in defeat. "I was only able to make one visit back; when I attempted again to return, it was as if our worlds were suddenly impossibly far apart; no magic could span that gap."

"And... our shieldmates?" Trey reluctantly asked.

"Crossing the worlds was very difficult and it drained me badly. I lost consciousness when we arrived, and when I woke, I found only you."

Trey's heart fell. He had been nursing the hope that his shieldmates were near, that they would soon be reunited and they could return to their fight.

"How were you able to break my spell?" Trey asked.

"I didn't," Robin said, spreading their hands in confusion. "I had spent most of a year making attempts and failing. As far as I can tell, the woman who brought you here was somehow able to release you."

"Daniella is a powerful witch," Trey said solemnly, gesturing to her wondrous house and the one-way communication portal.

Robin opened their mouth, then closed it thoughtfully again without argument.

"There's more," they said with a sigh.

Trey didn't want more of this news. "Tell me," he commanded anyway.

"The veil is growing thin again. Cerad was able to make a portal through, big enough to send an advance force."

"Dours," Trey growled. "In *this* world."

"Dours at *least*," Robin said grimly.

Trey's mind swirled in dismay. The kingdoms had fallen. And they'd inadvertently brought their battle to Daniella's world. And no matter how powerful she was, no matter how great her technology, this world was not prepared for the enemy it now faced.

CHAPTER 6

*D*aniella wondered if she'd made a terrible mistake leaving Trey without supervision in her house.

He was clearly clueless about technology. Would he burn down her house trying to operate the stove? Or electrocute himself accidentally?

Part of her also felt like it was a terrible shame to leave that kind of gorgeous, helpless man alone, when he might need help *bathing*. Surely he'd need help turning on the hot water, and…

Daniella jerked her mind off that track as she arrived at the cafe. "Hi Marie!" she called as the door tinkled merrily behind her.

"You're late, Whitney Houston," Marie retorted coldly.

Daniella looked at the clock, baffled and more than a little hurt. She was maybe an entire minute behind schedule and the cafe was nearly deserted. Was Marie confused because Daniella usually arrived half an hour early to take lunch? But they'd talked about that on the phone… and it wasn't like Marie to use Daniella's old nickname, knowing how much it stung. Daniella didn't sing as she worked anymore.

Marie retreated back into the kitchen as Daniella stomped the snow from her shoes and hung up her coat.

Two regulars, Fred and Juan, were sitting together drinking coffee and two strangers were looking over menus. Daniella nodded at the former and went to take drink orders from the latter.

"I'm Daniella, I'll be your server today. Can I start you off with a beverage?" she offered cheerfully.

"I'm Linda," the woman introduced herself. "Diet cola."

"Frank," the man said. "Just ice water."

"Have you decided what to order or do you need a little more time?" Daniella asked.

They each picked hot sandwiches with special requests. "No problem at all," Daniella assured them. "Let me get this back to the kitchen and get those drinks."

Marie took the orders with uncharacteristic ill will and Daniella filled opaque plastic glasses with ice cubes, water, and cola.

She thought she felt something twine around her ankles like a cat, but when she looked down, she didn't see anything there.

A curious feeling crept up her legs, like she'd just stepped into freezing cold water, like something was whispering in her ears, trying to make her feel afraid and angry and unsettled. "I don't have time for this," she said to her legs, and the sensation and the pressing insecurities were gone as quickly as they had come on. She was just Daniella again.

When she went back out to the restaurant, Fred and Juan were arguing heatedly. Daniella put the drinks down in front of the visitors. "Are you folks headed somewhere for Christmas?" she asked conversationally.

"Visiting family," Frank answered.

"*His* family," Linda laughed. "We're looking forward to one of those absurd spreads with all the trimmings and a fat turkey."

They talked for a while about Christmas food; Daniella confessed to her tiny fruitcake and they all chuckled about how terrible they were, and how pretty, and how they ought to taste as good as they looked.

When she came back with their sandwiches, the argument between Fred and Juan had escalated, and Daniella served the couple more quickly than she usually would and excused herself to see if she could defuse it.

"Can I refill your coffee?" she offered peacefully.

Just then, she heard the jangle of the bell at the door and Marie's voice, angry and full of spite. "What are you doing here? You aren't welcome here!"

Daniella turned in surprise to see Marie standing with a skillet in her hand, glaring at the new customer, Angie, the local doctor's receptionist.

"I just need..." Angie started

"I told you no pickles!" Linda suddenly said stridently.

"Damn, Linda, are you going to be this picky with my mother?" Frank snarled back. "You could just take them off, you don't have to abuse the staff like you abuse everyone else in your life."

"I was hoping for one last meal that was decent before we had to eat your mother's greasy, over-cooked crap. And it's rich of *you* to call *me* abusive." Linda had a butter knife in her hand and looked as though she might use it.

"Get out of my restaurant, stranger, I won't have you here!" Marie hollered at the stunned young woman at the door.

Which was when Fred stood up and decked Juan.

It wasn't a good hit, being across the table, but Daniella startled backwards in surprise, spilling hot coffee over her hand and crying out in pain.

Everyone paused for a moment, looking dazed, and Danilla put the coffee pot down on the table firmly as she used her apron to dab the hot coffee from her hand and wrist.

"I need all of you to stop this right now," she said firmly, pitching her voice to carry.

"Fred, Juan has been your friend for twenty years. You apologize to him and fix whatever nonsense this is. Juan, you'll accept that apology and you'll both move on. You got it?"

She didn't wait for their acknowledgment, turning furiously to the couple. "Two minutes ago, you were looking forward to a Christmas dinner with your family. Family that you *love* and are excited to see again. You were holding hands across the table. Find that place again," she demanded.

Then she rounded on Marie. "You know Angie. She's been here a dozen times before, and you have never had the slightest problem with her. I don't know what's wrong with you, but it is Christmas Eve and I am not going to put up with crazy when there should be carols and goodwill."

She was watching Marie as she spoke and Daniella could have sworn she watched a film of darkness fall away from her boss's face.

Marie put a hand to her lips, looking deeply confused. "I don't know what came over me," she said, glancing at Angie in confused horror and dropping her gaze in embarrassment. "I'm… so sorry."

Fred was apologizing to Juan more profusely than Daniella would have guessed he was capable of, and Juan stood to draw Fred into a gruff, manly, embarrassed embrace as they both tried to take the blame for the argument that neither one of them could really seem to remember.

"I love your mother's cooking," Linda was telling her husband in shock. "I don't understand. I was just... so angry."

"You aren't abusive," Frank assured her. "I've never thought so in my life."

Daniella took her scalded hand back to the kitchen to run cold water over it, and when she returned, Marie was chatting merrily with Angie at the cashier's stand.

"Oh, Daniella, Angie just came by to ask for a cup of sugar for a recipe. The grocer closed early and we're one of the last places open. Be a dear and make her a to-go bag for me, will you?"

Daniella looked around the room curiously. Fred and Juan were chatting lazily over their coffee again. The strange couple was commenting on some of the local photos that were hanging in the cafe. None of them seemed to even *remember* their irrational outbursts. Only Angie appeared to notice anything out of the ordinary, and she exchanged a baffled shoulder shrug with Daniella.

"Sorry about the pickles," she told Linda as she brought her their bill.

Linda looked at her blankly and Daniella didn't press the issue. Marie must have turned the music back on; Christmas carols were playing over the sound system again.

Everyone tipped generously.

CHAPTER 7

Daniella's return was heralded by Fabio, who went to the door and began whining and swirling in an excited dance. It took Trey a moment to realize what he was trying to convey.

Daniella opened the door and came in cautiously. She stared at Trey as she absently patted Fabio. "I thought maybe I'd imagined you," she said frankly.

"I assure you, I am flesh and blood," Trey said, looking down at the gleaming noble shirt she'd lent him.

She blushed and handed him a bag. "I stopped by the second hand store. They weren't technically open, but I have a key and left cash. These should… er… fit you better."

Upon inspection, the bag was filled with clothing that was no less strange than what he was wearing, but considerably less sparkly. Wearing the unicorn crest was probably above his station. "My thanks."

"I'll just take Fabio out for a moment while you change," she offered, and Fabio followed her eagerly out the door.

"That's your witch, then?" Robin asked, buzzing down from above the door.

"Not mine," Trey said regretfully as he shed the pale garments. The new clothing was plain, in dark colors, but it fit much better. She had even thought to bring a pair of boots, a second pair of socks, and undergarments in a battered clear package. There was a light jacket that had clearly seen better days.

There was a shy knock on the door shortly after he'd changed and Trey opened it.

"I wasn't sure if you'd be done dressing," Daniella explained. The chill outside would explain the catch to her breath, though Trey wondered briefly whether she might be as captured by him as he was by her. "You... look great. Er, better. I mean, it looks like I guessed your size right."

"My thanks," Trey said soberly, but Daniella was staring past him now as Fabio pushed into the room, filling the room with his wagging tail.

"Is that... a fairy on my kitchen table?"

"This is my teacher, Robin. They are a fable."

"And I swear that if you call me Tinkerbell, I will curse you with pimples that would make puberty quail," they added.

"This day could not get weirder," Daniella said, shaking her head. "I'm... just going to roll with this, too. Have you had dinner?" She edged around Trey into the kitchen, then paused. "Do you... eat food?" she asked Robin.

"Do you have pizza?" Robin asked hopefully.

"Yeah, I'll start the oven," Daniella agreed. She went to the fridge, opened a drawer in the bottom, and withdrew a circular frozen slab. "And that's probably a good choice because I was kind of running low on flower nectar and morning dew."

Robin laughed at this, though Trey didn't understand the joke.

Daniella slipped into her back room and emerged dressed in clothing very similar to Trey's new garb: dark heather blue pants of some thick material, and a black t-shirt. Hers had a stylized gold bat across her chest, which didn't help Trey resist his desire to stare there.

The cube with the pots on top gave a little beep and Daniella opened a door to the front of it that released a wave of heat. She unwrapped the frozen circle and placed it inside.

Daniella did something arcane with the numbers above, then turned to face them with her arms crossed. "I have questions," she said boldly.

"I will answer them to the best of my abilities," Trey said solemnly.

Robin flitted to sit on the kitchen counter.

Daniella stabbed a finger in his direction. "You're… not a fairy?"

"A fable," Robin corrected. "A creature made of magic rather than flesh."

"Sure," Daniella said. "Okay, I can handle that if I can handle anything." She turned her brown-eyed gaze to Trey. "And you, you're…a dragon knight. But you're human right now."

"This is my human form," Trey agreed. "I can shift between them at will."

"But you're too big to shift here."

"I would damage your dwelling," Trey said regretfully. He desperately wanted to show her his dragon form, even if he wasn't sure why he wanted so badly to impress her.

"We'll come back to that," Daniella said wryly. "Next question, where are you from? Or…when? And why are you here?"

"I can answer some of that," Robin volunteered. "I've been here long enough to figure a few things out. We're from what you might call a parallel universe, one with more magic, less technology. Our world was being conquered by darkness and we were... part of an elite group of fighters trying to forestall the inevitable."

"It was not inevitable," Trey growled.

Daniella ignored him. "Conquered by darkness is a little dramatic, don't you think?"

Robin shrugged one of their shoulders. "It's accurate. The dours, in particular, leave a darkness over the mortals that they touch. It's palpable."

"Dours?"

"They're like... footsoldiers of the evil that we fight," Robin said. "The first wave that our enemy sends in. They are insidious and devastating, their touch bringing out the very worst in human nature. Good people are suddenly angry, greedy, fearful, turning against each other without reason or thought. Dours flow into a community and by the time they are done with it, families have dissolved, neighbors are feuding, and churches are burning each other."

Daniella's eyes were large and alarmed. "What...what do they look like?"

"Shadows," Trey supplied. "Like dark shades scuttling away out of the corners of your eyes."

"I saw one," she murmured. "At work this afternoon, it was... it was terrible. Like no one was themselves, like they were suddenly suspicious and judgmental of each other. And I watched that darkness drop out of Marie's face, like someone took a mask off of her. When I was cleaning up later, I thought I saw a black cat slipping out of the kitchen, but I never got a good look at it."

"Dours," Robin and Trey agreed grimly.

"When a person has the darkness on them, we say they are ridden," Trey added. "They are not themselves."

"Why are there dours in *my* world?" Daniella demanded. "Did you bring them here?"

Trey and the little winged figure wearing doll clothing glanced at each other, looking guilty.

"They appear to have followed us," Robin said regretfully.

"From another world," Daniella said flatly. "Now, wait, you said these things are the first wave that an *enemy* sends in. What enemy is this?"

"Cerad," Trey growled.

"Who's Cerad?"

Robin answered, "A powerful man from my world, one who learned how to control the dours for his own purposes, breed them, and spread them to do his will. He feeds on chaos and destruction, and would not… did not… rest until the kingdom was at his feet. I fear he has designs on your world next."

"Designs?" Daniella whispered.

"Your world is rich and innocent," Robin said. "It must be irresistible to someone like Cerad. And it would appear that the veil between our worlds is getting thin enough again for him to punch through."

Daniella stared at them. "There are more of these things?"

Robin tried to reassure her, "The veil is still strong. I do not think he can get more than a few dours through now without great effort. He is only testing the waters now; we have time."

Daniella rubbed a hand wearily over her eyes. "Is it possible to get to the point where I'm just too tired *not* to believe you?"

Trey swiftly turned to get her a chair. "Lady Daniella,

we have imposed on you terribly and I feel responsible for the introduction of the dours to your helpless world. Please, sit. Do not exert yourself further on our behalf."

Daniella was still standing, looking perplexedly at the chair he was holding out, when there was a demanding beep from the woodless oven.

She turned away, instead, and used a heavy mitten to remove the slab, no longer frozen. It steamed now and had turned a golden brown, with sizzling cheese over the top. "Let's all sit," she suggested, cutting it with a spinning knife and placing slices on plates.

Robin's slice was just a sliver and they awkwardly sat with their back against the wall while Daniella and Trey sat opposite each other at the table. "Careful," she cautioned. "It's hot."

Trey managed to scorch the top of his mouth despite her warning, but the delicious food was worth the temporary pain. Apparently, Daniella agreed, eating swiftly and sucking breath in to cool her mouth.

"Tell me again about the dour attack," Robin commanded, and Daniella unfolded the tale with more detail.

"Oh, you know," she said thoughtfully. "I was alone in the kitchen before that all happened and I felt the strangest sensation... like I'd just stepped into ice water and my legs were numb and I was really weirdly angry about it."

Trey let his breath hiss in. "But you escaped its influence." Because clearly, Daniella was not in thrall to a dour, feeding strangers as she was, rather than pitching them out into the snow. "What did you do?"

Daniella looked as confused as he felt. "I just... I just thought that I didn't have time for this, and it went away."

"You are indeed a powerful witch," Trey said in awe.

She squirmed in her chair. "Trey, I'm not a witch. I

know that a lot of this stuff looks magical, but it's just technology. I work a job, earn money, and buy these things to make my life easier. There's no magic to it at all."

Trey was dubious of this claim. She was clearly unaware of the glamour she was casting even now, making him long to kneel at her feet and pledge his everything to her.

Robin, lifting a piece of their pizza that was almost as long as their arm span, paused. "What I don't understand is how the others in the restaurant escaped the thrall. Even if Daniella was somehow immune—which some humans are, but precious few—how did the rest of them get free?"

Hope rose in Trey's chest. "Our shieldmates?"

"It sounds like their work," Robin agreed cautiously. "But I would know if they were nearby. I've been dowsing for them."

"All I did was point out that they were all being crazy and told them to stop it," Daniella said, shrugging. "How do *you* fight these things?"

"As they are darkness, we are light," Trey tried to explain.

"You all, you're like wizards or something?" Daniella suggested. "Good wizards?"

"Wizards and witches make power with spells and potions," Trey clarified. "We *are* power. The power of light."

Daniella gave him a look that Trey had trouble identifying. Like she desperately wanted to believe him but couldn't quite. "Like…angels?"

Robin gave a dry laugh. "Like…and not like," they said. "You might say *fae*, from what I've read. I am all magic, the knights are half-magic."

"What's an angel?" Trey asked. "Wait, when a bell

rings, an angel gets its wings." The puzzling Christmas play had featured one. "They are advisors of good?"

"Don't listen to too much television," Robin suggested wryly. "It'll rot your brain."

"I warned him," Daniella said sideways to Robin as she stood to retrieve more pizza. "Want another slice, Clarence?"

Clarence. The angel. Wait, she meant *him*. She was teasing him. "Yes, Lady, at your will." She met his eyes and blushed.

The slice she dropped on his plate was not as sizzling hot, but every bit as delectable. Robin polished off their own slice, nearly the size of their entire body, and brushed their hands off. "I'm going to check out the cafe, see if I can find any trace of your shieldmates, and track the dours." They fluttered to Trey. "I regret having to leave you so soon, but I can travel and investigate faster alone. There are some advantages to this size. I will be back when I can."

They briefly touched foreheads, Robin's head tiny against Trey's.

"When you return, we will find the others and make plans for returning to our world," Trey said firmly. Then there was a brief split in the air and Robin was gone.

CHAPTER 8

Daniella decided that dragon knights and *dours* and disappearing fairies were basically exhausting. "It's getting late. I… ah… usually take Fabio out for a walk right before bed, do you want to come with?"

"You should have a companion, to protect you," Trey said formally.

Daniella suspected that this was the point a good feminist would protest that she could protect herself, thank you very much. But she was tired and frankly a little afraid. It had been terribly alarming to watch her friends and neighbors turn on each other. So she put on her jacket, found an extra hat, scarf, and mittens for Trey, and they went outside.

Fabio bolted to the end of his leash, smelling and marking everything. Daniella led them to the little park at the center of town where she could let Fabio run and trust that he would come back.

In the mess of magic and strange beings, she had forgotten that it was Christmas Eve and it all came rushing back to her when she realized how *quiet* everything was. All the businesses had closed and the streets were empty. There was a little slushy snow left in sheltered places, and there was a chill to the air that made Daniella tuck her scarf in a little tighter.

She wasn't entirely surprised when Trey carefully took her hand and pulled it into his elbow. They had to walk very close together, linked that way, and it took a moment or two to perfect their strides so that they were walking in harmony.

Fabio ran out ahead of them joyously and Daniella was all warm where Trey was up against her side while her face was a contrast of cold. It began to snow, with fat, slow flakes that lingered on their scarves and mittens. When she slipped Fabio off his leash at the park, a streak of mischief made her bend and scoop up a puny handful of snow.

Trey, suspecting nothing, took the sad snowball in the face and his face split into a gorgeous, unexpected grin as he bent to gather his own ammunition.

They chased around the park, dodging swings and using the slide as protection from flying snowballs. Fabio ran and frolicked with them, eagerly chasing the balls as the snow fell thicker and thicker.

Daniella slipped in the slushy snow, nearly falling, and Trey caught her by the hand at the last moment and drew her close. For a lingering, blissful moment, she thought he was going to kiss her.

Then Fabio stuck his nose in between them and tried to lick her face, which was not at all the kiss she was hoping for.

Their walk back was quieter, but no less close, and Daniella wondered at her desire and longing. It wasn't like her to swoon over a pretty face. She was practical. Self-sufficient.

But if there could be magic in the world, and fairy-like

fables, and dragon-knights, could there be love at first sight? Could Trey be the person she had always told herself she wasn't really waiting for?

Then Fabio went into pointer mode, which always looked awkward on his long Afghan body and he began to dance eagerly at the end of his leash.

"Hello, Daniella!" her neighbor Anna called. "Hello, Fabio!"

Her cheerful voice put to ease a fear Daniella hadn't even known she had been carrying with her: that others in her sleepy town might be in the chill grip of the dours even now.

"Hi, Anna!" Daniella called in return. "Hello, Ambergris."

Out of long habit, they approached to let their dogs catch up and sniff each other curiously. Anna gave Trey a long, appraising look.

"Oh, this is Trey," Daniella said, blushing and glad that it was dark here, away from the scattered street lights. "This is Anna," she said carefully. "My neighbor."

Trey bowed courteously over Anna's hand, causing her to grin. He did not, Daniella noticed, offer to kiss it and she was jealously glad. "I am delighted to meet you, neighbor of Daniella's."

"Santa Claus certainly brought you a delightful gift," Anna teased shamelessly.

"Oh, he's, ah, just…" Daniella had no way to finish the sentence.

"Did you meet Daniella on one of those dating sites?" Anna guessed, addressing Trey.

Trey gave Daniella a sideways glance begging for help. Daniella shrugged helplessly and Trey plowed forward. "Yes, certainly. It was a very good place for dating and we are spending Christmas Eve together.

Waiting for Santa and choirs of angels. It's a wonderful life."

Anna giggled and Daniella had to join her. "Well, I won't keep you kids," Anna said with a knowing wink for Daniella. "Good to see you, Fabio."

They patted one another's dogs and Daniella was grateful to cross the street and go up the walk to her own house. The steady snow had already started to drift and was already a fluffy inch deep along the sidewalk.

The house was warm after the chill of outdoors and Daniella shook the snow from her boots. Trey surprised her by unwrapping her scarf for her, and she returned the favor by helping him remove his hat without dumping all the snow down his back.

He had the dreamiest hair, just longer than shoulder length, and more fabulous by far even than Fabio's. Either Fabio.

I'd buy any butter he tried to sell me, Daniella thought, trying not to giggle.

"So, I thought you could sleep in my bed," she blurted, only hearing how her words might be taken after they were out of her mouth. "By yourself, I mean. I would sleep on the couch. But the couch is too short for you, and it wouldn't be comfortable. So you should take the bed. My bed. To sleep. Not with me."

Brilliant, Daniella assured herself. *A true show of intelligence and wit.*

"You have honored me with your hospitality," Trey said quietly. "I could not impose."

"It's not an imposition," Daniella hastened to assure him. "It's... ah, local tradition. You would insult me if you slept on the couch."

Trey didn't entirely look like he believed her, his eyes warm and green and sparkling. But he didn't argue.

Daniella showed him the bathroom and demonstrated the sink and toilet, emphasizing that the seat and lid needed to be put down after use. "Fabio, for all of his stunning good looks, has the intelligence of a goldfish, and he'll drink out of the toilet if you give him the chance. It makes a terrible mess, and stepping in cold toilet-water-dog-spit is not my idea of a fun way to start the morning."

She shut him in the bathroom while she ransacked her room, picking up all the drifting piles of clothing in various states of clean and putting them all haphazardly in the closet, trying to tidy the books and make it look less like a disaster zone and more like the well-ordered bedroom of someone respectable. She started trying to hide the dirty romance books, then realized it was a completely lost cause. Maybe he wouldn't know what they were.

Once it started to look somewhat better, Daniella realized she needed to put clean sheets on, dismantled the bed, and remade it with the only clean sheets she had: mermaids. The dirty sheets were wadded into the closet and firmly shut behind the door.

Would he look in the bedside drawer? Daniella finally decided that it would serve him right if he did and emerged from the bedroom to find that Trey was standing before the Christmas tree, frowning thoughtfully at the fragile ornament that had been hung back up on a branch.

A dragon.

Was it even possible?

He was so glorious, even as a human. But Daniella wasn't sure, even after this day of impossible things, if she could believe in *dragons*.

"So, there you go," she said nervously. "Clean sheets, I've left you one of the pillows." She had the other pillow and an armful of spare blankets. "I'll be completely comfortable on the couch."

It occurred to her, rather suddenly, that she was letting a complete stranger, a total unknown, sleep in her house with her. In her bed. Even if she wasn't in it with him. And oh, she wanted to be in that bed, wanted to know what his kiss would do to her mouth after the thrill that it had been on her knuckles.

It was reckless. It was *stupid*. It was the headline of a sensational article. Maybe they'd call him 'The Christmas Eve Killer.'

And when he lifted her hands to his lips for another of those chaste, knee-melting kisses, Daniella didn't even care.

"Thank you," he said simply. "Thank you for... so much."

Then he went to the bedroom, shut the door, and Daniella was left to lie down on the couch and get a face full of Fabio tongue until she could get herself together enough to push him away.

She fell asleep long before she thought it would be possible.

CHAPTER 9

*D*espite Daniella's decadent soft bed and crisp linens, Trey slept poorly. He tossed and turned, thinking about the brave tilt to her chin, the brightness of her eyes. Her hair looked so… soft and touchable. Like the curves of her lush body.

It had been a long time since he had energy to spare to think about lying with a woman and arguably, he should not allow himself to be distracted now. Not with dours infesting her world.

He heard Daniella rise from the couch at last and begin to do something in the kitchen that involved metallic clanking. The front door opened and shut twice, with noisy dog sounds on either side that indicated Fabio's brief release.

Trey cautiously opened the door to Daniella's inner chamber.

"Merry Christmas!" Daniella called from the kitchen. "I made pancakes!"

She was wearing her hair back in a long, thick tail and she had a spatula in one hand.

"Merry Christmas," Trey replied, mystified.

Daniella's imperious spatula directed him to sit at the kitchen table and he did so obediently. "Is this a traditional holiday meal?" he asked.

"Oh, I don't know about generally traditional," Daniella said as she put a plate in front of him. "But my parents always made blueberry pancakes on Christmas morning. I think it was mostly to bribe us to wait to open presents until the evening. Every family does it a little differently. My best friend always got to open her presents in the morning."

"Your parents, are they no longer living?" It seemed strange that Daniella would live alone.

"Oh, they're still alive. They moved to Florida for retirement last year. This is my first Christmas solo. That's why the tree doesn't have any ornaments... except for yours. For now. I mean, that's obviously *yours*." She put a pile of flat circular cakes speckled with round dark spots on the plate before him.

"I'm not certain I follow that logic," Trey confessed. Daniella put a plate of her own pancakes on the table and sat opposite from him, demonstrating how to smother them in syrup and cut them with a fork.

"Mmmm..." Daniella said. Around a mouthful, she added, "Ornaments in our family are supposed to be meaningful. I mean, anyone can go buy some glass balls or plastic Santa Clauses, but our tree was always covered with memories. Each ornament came with a story—the first Christmas my parents had together, that year we went to Egypt for the holidays, the year my sister was born. Trimming the tree was like paging through a photo album. I wanted to have a tree like that."

Trey got a sticky mouthful of the cake into his mouth. "This is blissful," he said in awe. "What are the berries?"

"Blueberries! We picked these ourselves in the mountains two autumns ago. They've been in my freezer waiting for a special occasion."

"Is this a special occasion?" Trey asked innocently.

Daniella gazed across the table at him. "Yes," she said softly. Then color crept up her cheeks and she looked away. "I mean, because it's Christmas! Biggest holiday of the year!"

"You have many holidays?" Trey asked, wondering at the look she'd given him.

"We like to celebrate things," she said, still embarrassed. Then she looked up sharply. "Don't you have holidays?"

Trey frowned. "It has been… a long time since we had anything to celebrate," he said gently.

"It's not your fault," Daniella said softly. "You can't save the world alone."

"My shieldmates…"

"Even five of you can't be expected to save an entire world."

Trey gazed at her solemnly, trying to figure out how to explain how he believed they *had* to be enough.

"Will you show me?"

Trey looked at her in confusion.

"Your dragon, will you show me? There's a place we can drive, where no one goes. Especially on Christmas."

Trey bowed his head. "Yes," he agreed. "I would like that. Very much."

When he had finished his pancakes, Daniella loaded their dirty dishes into another of her technology cubes and set it to rumble and hiss. They dressed in their outside garments, to Fabio's great excitement, and walked out into a snowy wonderland. There was a scant inch of snow, glittering in the early sun like the unicorn shirt she had lent him.

Daniella led him around her house to a back road and began brushing off a strange contraption.

"Oh, yes," Trey remembered as it was uncovered. "Rock bottom prices!"

Daniella looked at him in outrage, then burst out laughing. "I really shouldn't have made television your introduction to my world," she said with chagrin. "Load up, Fabio."

Trey, strapped carefully into the machine, was awed by their breath-taking journey. Fabio was only barely less excited than he was, especially when Daniella showed Trey how to put the window down.

"This is amazing!" he crowed, craning his head out the window until the shoulder strap held him back.

"You should sit down and roll that up," Daniella scolded him.

Trey promptly sat and returned the glass to its original position. "Is it unsafe?"

"Not unsafe, just cold!" Daniella laughed at him. She looked at him sideways. "It's nice to see you smile."

The mention of it made Trey aware of his own unfamiliar expression. "It's easy to smile with you," he said honestly, remembering their impromptu snow battle, and the breathless hope in her face when he caught her from falling.

He'd almost kissed her.

He'd wanted to kiss her.

He hadn't stopped wanting to kiss her.

He wasn't sure he could ever stop wanting to kiss her.

But what kind of offering was *his* kiss?

They came to a quiet drive through dense evergreens, and Daniella pulled up in front of a house of two stories, sided in rich red-painted wood with white trim.

"This was my folks' house," she said. "It's still on the

market, so no one should bother us here and I have a key if we get cold. Though now that I think of it, I'm not actually sure the power is hooked up."

There was a large, bright clear space before the house, and the area all around was fringed with tall, dark trees that provided privacy. "This will do fine," Trey said approvingly. There was room here to take off, if he chose to, and at the least, he'd be able to spread his wings and show her the true glory of his green wingspan.

Fabio bolted from the car door as soon as it was opened and made a wide circuit of the yard while Trey paced to the center of the space.

"Am I far enough away?" Daniella asked nervously. "Should I park the car further to the side?"

"This is perfect," Trey assured her, and he closed his eyes to focus on his second form.

He was power and might, beauty and strength.

He gave a great sigh of satisfaction as his wings expanded and shivered as all his diamond-hard scales settled neatly into place.

He was a dragon!

Trey opened his eyes and looked up at Fabio.

He swirled in confusion, his claws cleaving through the thin layer of snow and his tail whipping behind him.

A giant Fabio fell to his front elbows, fringed tail wagging above him in clear play mode.

Trey spread his wings and bounced slightly into the air as he realized the problem.

He was the size of a cat.

CHAPTER 10

Trey's dragon was as beautiful as he was, all jewel-tones and shimmering scales, with diaphanous wings and a long, flexible tail tapering to a beautiful fan. He looked like a dragon out of a fairy tale book, with bright eyes in a wedge-shaped head on a graceful neck. His mouth showed razor-sharp teeth and he had claws like knives on every foot.

Tiny knives the size of the tips of cuticle scissors.

Daniella had been braced for a towering form, sure that he would be huge and terrifying. She spent the moments before Trey transformed silently reminding herself not to scream.

Instead, he was the size of a glittery chicken, and he was so surprised by his own size that he nearly fell over.

Fabio was not going to let an opportunity to play pass him by and he gave an eager yelp of joy and dashed at Trey's dragon form, darting aside at the last moment to bound around in a spiral of energy, spraying snow everywhere. Daniella belatedly considered that it might not be entirely safe for him to play with a fire-breathing dragon no matter what his size was. Dog fur was flammable, and Fabio had a lot of it!

"Fabio, leave it!"

Fabio was too wound up to listen, and came barreling back into tiny-dragon-Trey.

They tumbled together, Trey too slow to react and Fabio too excited to stop himself. Dragon wings spread wide, and there was a tangle of paws and tails and then Trey was sitting up as a human and Fabio was absolutely sure that he was hiding the new play-thing behind him, nosing and sniffing and trying to burrow underneath him in the snow.

"Fabio, Fabio, leave it!" Daniella choked back her laugh at the absurdity of all of it.

Utterly befuddled, Fabio whined and cocked his head at Trey, who patted him solemnly on the head and climbed to his feet looking dazed.

"I was…much smaller than I expected," he said in chagrin, while Fabio chased around with his nose in the snow trying to track down the mysterious creature. "That was very alarming."

"You were adorable!" Daniella said.

"I was sadly diminished," Trey said in outrage. "I promise you, I am much larger than that!"

"No, really," Daniella said, trying very hard not to giggle. "Size doesn't matter. It's fine. I'm not disappointed." They were things she never thought she'd have to say to a man she hadn't even slept with.

Daniella pulled the corners of her mouth down with effort; she really did feel bad for him, but she still found it all terrifically funny.

Even desperately pouting, the man was gorgeous.

"It must be as Robin warned," Trey growled. "The leylines here are cloudy. Magic is weaker here, different."

"You know what would cheer you up?" Daniella prompted.

Trey muttered something that Daniella couldn't quite make out about dismembering enemies and feasting on... something.

"A milkshake," Daniella said. "There's this great little truck stop just a few miles up the twenty and I bet you dollars to donuts that they're open today. I was planning to make a big early dinner, and a milkshake is just what we need to get us through to that."

Trey gave a frustrated sigh. "I don't know what half of that meant, but I will trust your judgment."

Daniella loaded a reluctant Fabio back into the car and buckled Trey into his seat. She drove out of the driveway and turned north. "So, what happens to your clothing when you change shapes?" she asked, hoping to distract him from his sulk.

"It is... part of who we are at that moment, so the magic changes it with us."

"And if you're holding something?"

"I'd still be holding it in the new shape," Trey said shortly.

"What if you were wearing something like... a backpack?"

"Like a knapsack? Best hope that it was sized for a dragon." This only served to remind Trey about his new, undignified size and he went back to a silent sulk that none of Daniella's questions could rouse him from. She put on a radio station playing classic Christmas songs and after a time could not help but sing along.

Trey gave her a sideways look, halfway through a rendition of a traditional. "You have a beautiful voice," he said admiringly.

Not good enough, Daniella thought, but she didn't say

anything, pushing the memories aside. She stopped singing.

By the time they had arrived at Rosa's, she had mostly coaxed him back to cheer and had failed badly to explain some of the traditional songs. Santa Claus was just weird when you tried to describe him. Rudolph was every bit as bad.

But then, she was driving for Christmas milkshakes at a truck stop with a fae man from another dimension who could change into a dragon.

A dragon the size of a cat, true, but it was still an impressive feat.

Rosa's was, fortunately, open for business, and there were even a few big shipping trucks in the lot. Daniella's car looked very small in comparison and Trey outright stared at them before they went in.

"Your world has many wonders," he said, shaking his head. "That you can manage such things without magic…"

But there was definitely magic afoot inside Rosa's.

Now that she knew what she was seeing, Daniella recognized the unmistakable fingerprints of the dours over everyone inside.

Two truckers were circling each other, already bloodied from their fight. A waitress was throwing a pitcher at a cowering customer and the cook was smashing something to pieces in the open kitchen beyond the counter.

To Daniella's astonishment, Trey leaped for the nearest table and flung himself into the air, shifting as he went. His wings were twice his length and the whoosh of air from his downbeat blew Daniella's hair back from her face. He deftly cornered and flew like an arrow towards the fighting truckers.

Daniella was frozen, not sure what he was going to do,

when he opened his mouth and a gush of silver flame washed forward in his path to spill over the combatants. Daniella wanted to shriek at him not to hurt them, remembering how her friends had been able to shake away the dour's grips... but the flame didn't hurt them, or light anything on fire, or feel at all hot from this distance.

Instead, it seemed to burn away the darkness that had settled over the truckers. Daniella had the weirdest impression that she was watching ash fall away from the two men as they shook themselves and stepped back.

Trey was already diving for the waitress and the customer. He was sweeping down on them with his not-really-flame blazing before him when the cook emerged from the kitchen holding a huge cleaver, vaulting over the counter directly at Daniella with a blood-curdling scream of rage.

Trey was too committed to help her in time, and for some reason, it simply didn't occur to her to turn and run.

"No!" she said firmly, projecting her voice, and the cook stopped in his tracks, knife upheld.

"This isn't who you are!" Daniella reminded him, and the mask of rage over his face cracked to reveal a puzzled man who slowly put down his weapon and wandered back to the kitchen in a daze, shaking his head.

Trey, his work with the waitress and the fearful customer finished, landed at her side and shifted back into his human shape. No one seemed to find this the slightest bit remarkable and all of them were returning to their usual roles as if nothing had happened.

The waitress was laughing over the broken pitcher. "I'll be right with you folks!" she called.

Trey turned to Daniella and unexpectedly enfolded her into his arms. "I didn't think I could get to you in time," he said, sounding choked. "How did you stop him?"

"I... just spoke to him," Daniella said in confusion. "I said... 'No.' And 'This isn't who you are.'"

"Is that what you did with the people at your place of employment?"

Trey hadn't offered to let go of her and Daniella was finding that his chest was a perfectly wonderful place to be crushed. "Yes?"

"You are indeed powerful," Trey said in wonder. "I have never seen the like in a mortal before."

She was trembling from the adrenaline and he stroked her hair. "You burned the darkness from them," she could finally say.

She felt his arms tighten. "I could have burned the darkness from an entire town in a matter of moments, at my true size. Now I can barely contain an ill-attended eatery."

Daniella gave a choking breath that was almost a sob.

"Er, can I get you folks something?" the waitress asked hesitantly.

Trey reluctantly let go of Daniella and she just as reluctantly stepped out of the comforting circle of his arms. "Milkshakes," she said in a shaky voice. "Two, chocolate, to go." She didn't want to stay here.

"Sure thing," the waitress said cheerily. "Merry Christmas, by the way."

Right. Christmas.

Merry.

Trey's hand was in her own, somehow, and Daniella knew that it was exactly where it belonged.

CHAPTER 11

Daniella's house was beginning to feel like home. Trey desperately missed his shieldmates and wondered what had happened to them, but walking into the small dwelling filled him with a cozy contentment that he had never known before.

Daniella herself had rallied. Their chocolate milkshakes had been as delicious as she had promised, and the ride home had been filled with more nonsensical Christmas music that Daniella hadn't entirely been able to resist singing along with, though whenever she caught herself, she stopped.

"I love the snow!" she insisted as she unlocked the door and Fabio bravely went ahead to check for intruders. "We call this a white Christmas, and all of them should be. Next, I'm going to introduce you to eggnog, and we're going to have a proper Christmas dinner, and oh! I got you a present."

"A present?"

"A gift. Christmas has sort of turned into this holiday of a billion quirky traditions and one of the more universal ones is the idea that you give the people you care about a small present to express your... affection."

"Do you have affection for me?" Trey asked before he could stop himself. Even before he had finished speaking, he knew it had been a mistake. It was too much to ask. He was a stranger in her world and she surely must think him unbearably needy.

He felt needy. Like he needed her touch, and her glance, and her voice. Like no shieldmate had ever felt so close, or so *real*.

Daniella blushed scarlet and refused to meet his eyes as she pulled off her cold jacket. "I... ah... have a ham to put in the oven. It's already cooked, it just needs to heat up. And I have to figure out how to cook yams. Christmas is as much about cooking as anything else, and I thought I ought to at least cook *something* from scratch."

"May I assist you?" Trey offered.

"I'd... I'd like that," she said, and she smiled a slow smile full of shy desire that made Trey's heart lift.

Together, they peeled yams and chopped them into pieces and placed them in a dish with squishy sugary cylinders according to a recipe that Daniella produced. "This was always my favorite part of Christmas," she sighed, putting them into the woodless oven with the ham.

"The food?" Trey asked.

"The cooking. With family."

It was another awkward moment as both of them realized that they weren't really family.

"This calls for eggnog," Daniella said. Then she added, "Because, I have to call my mother."

She poured them both foamy drinks that were less sweet and yet more rich than the milkshakes had been. Trey recognized the tang of alcohol underlying the flavor. When she explained its composition, he thought he could taste the egg in the blend.

Daniella took a deep breath after a few sips. "Give me about twenty minutes. I have to make this call now that I'm fortified."

The small box she produced—a *phone*—was clearly a method of communication; Trey remembered her talking to someone else through it the day before. She did something with it and then held it to the side of her face.

"Hi Mom!" she said cheerfully. "You guys eating dinner yet?"

She was quiet for a long time, with distant noises clearly connected with a string of conversation from the other end. She interjected a few things like, "That sounds like Carrie!" and "I bet it's wonderful," and "You'll have to send me a picture. Ask Dad how to do that."

She said proudly, "Yes, I've got a ham and some yams in the oven. We're going to have a real Christmas meal."

Her face turned beet red.

"Yeah, I've... uh... got a friend over."

"No," she insisted. "Just a friend. We just met."

Then she whispered in despair. "Moooooom."

And finally, "Let me say hi to Dad. I love you. Merry Christmas."

Her father apparently had something to say that made the color in her cheeks rise further.

"No... It's not... You know how Mom is... She'll be asking if we're engaged tomorrow... Yeah."

He also received a warm "I love you," and "Merry Christmas."

Then she removed the phone from her ear and pressed a symbol to turn it off. "I'm sorry," she said tearfully. "Just... you know. Family. They're so unbelievably nosy."

"My shieldmates were like that," Trey said quietly. "Nosy and well-meaning and so dear to my heart."

He was not sure what would have happened next if the beeping alarm on the oven hadn't gone off then.

"Oh!" Daniella said, wiping her eyes as surreptitiously as she could. "Dinner!"

There were so many dishes that the counter was crowded and their plates were heaping. Trey ate so much, of so many fascinating dishes that, by the end, he was groaning and holding his stomach.

"So delicious," Daniella moaned. "So full…"

"Is this normal?" Trey asked. "To feel like your jelly-bowl-bellied Santa Claus?"

"This is exactly right," Daniella assured him. "This is *perfect*."

After they put the copious quantities of leftovers into an already full fridge, they retired to the couch, to lean on each other comfortably and digest their food while they watched another Christmas play on the *television* called *A Miracle on 34th Street*. They started it halfway through and Daniella caught him up on what had already happened and answered his doltish questions about the setting and background.

Just as Trey was starting to feel that his meal was no longer taking up the bulk of his body, the play ended and Daniella turned it off.

She gave Fabio a large bone to gnaw. "Merry Christmas, mutt." Fabio whined in delight and went to a corner to wrap himself around it possessively.

"I got you something, too," Daniella told Trey. "I didn't have a chance to wrap it," she said apologetically. "But I saw it when I was getting your clothing and thought… you might enjoy it."

"You have given me so much already," Trey protested.

"I wanted to," Daniella said with a mysterious smile.

She vanished into her bedroom and emerged a few moments later. "Sit on the couch and close your eyes," she said, her voice full of mischief.

Trey did so, and felt Daniella sit beside him and deflect the couch. "Put your hands out!"

She placed an object into them and ordered him to open his eyes again.

"I... thought you might find this interesting. It reminded me of you."

It was a book of stories from her world, fairy tales, with amazingly fine, white paper and beautiful color illumination.

Daniella was watching him carefully as he turned it over in his hands, admiring the binding quality.

"You know, it didn't occur to me to ask if you could read," she said, looking suddenly nervous.

"Of course," Trey assured her. "We were well trained in literary and mathematical arts. This is beautiful."

Daniella's face bloomed into a happy smile. "I thought you would like it," she said warmly. "I hoped."

Trey had opened to an illustration of a knight bending down over a sleeping woman to kiss her.

Daniella blushed. "It is... a common theme in our stories that true love's kiss can break curses and evil spells," she said shyly.

"Is that how you freed me?" Trey had to ask.

Daniella didn't speak, but the catch to her breath was answer enough.

Trey set the book aside. "I have only one thing I can give you in return."

"You don't have to..." Daniella started to protest.

"The ornament I was trapped in. My curse. My prison."

"You can't give me that," Daniella insisted after a beat of surprise. "That's... well, it's sort of *you*."

Trey took her face in his hands, gently, carefully. "Then that's what I give you. All of me."

He didn't understand how a face could become that dear, that fast, how a person could get under his skin so completely. Her brown eyes were home.

He leaned in to kiss her at last.

CHAPTER 12

Daniella rose to meet Trey's mouth desperately, hardly daring to believe that this... this could be *hers*.

That glorious body, that expressive mouth, those soulful eyes... Daniella felt like she would break from the desire that was building in her. She wanted to touch every inch of his skin, to drink him in. She wanted... she wanted so much.

And Trey—beautiful, mysterious, powerful Trey—he wanted her, too.

He moaned in desperation when she broke off the kiss, but it was worth it when she peeled her shirt off over her head and his breath caught as he gazed at her in awe. Then he peeled his shirt off and Daniella returned the favor.

He was unbelievably built. Daniella had already observed that—she'd have to be blind not to notice how he filled up his shirts, even if she hadn't already ogled him naked. But now she got to touch him, to run her hands over all those knotty muscles and up his shoulders and down his arms and he was still staring at her like he wasn't sure what to do with his hands.

She unclipped her bra and slipped it off, then helpfully moved his hands to cup her breasts.

"Daniella," he murmured, and then he was kissing down her neck, lingering at her collarbone, his big hands caressing her, pulling her closer, desperately, cautiously, like he knew they might pass a point of no return.

And that suited her just *fine*.

He laid her back on the couch and when his bare chest brushed her breasts Daniella felt like her nipples were on fire. She could feel the bulk of his erection through his jeans as he straddled her, kissing her mouth again—more firmly this time.

She wrapped her arms around the mountains of his shoulders, arching up to rub herself against him as he took her bottom lip in his mouth and bit down, just hard enough to not-quite hurt.

Her arms drew back so she could get under his and she slipped her hands down to his waist. The pants she'd bought him were just a little large—for such a powerful man, he had very trim hips—and she could wriggle them down off of his butt cheeks without unbuttoning them as he continued to kiss her and caress her breasts and her sides. She couldn't reach far, pinned under him, but she could just get his ass free, cupping each cheek in an eager hand.

But it was what was on the other side, pressing against her, that she really wanted. She squirmed, pressing harder against him, and when he lifted for a moment, she shimmied out of her own jeans.

There was an urgent flurry of undressing, and then he was back on top of her, and this time there was nothing keeping them apart from each other.

She was wet, almost embarrassingly so, and when he teased at her entrance, Daniella spread her legs desperately and he slipped in with just enough friction to make her entire body light on fire.

She didn't realize she'd cried out until Fabio nosed her in the side, curious, concerned, and smelling of Christmas bone. "Get back," she ordered. When Trey stopped, confused, she took him with double handfuls of his gorgeous hair and told him, "Bedroom. Now!"

They scrambled for the bed, kicking the door shut on a puzzled Fabio.

At last, Trey was laying her down across the bedspread and there were kisses and touches and most of all, he was filling her, deliciously, the way that she'd wanted him to so badly.

She came in a blinding crest of pleasure and when she could think again, she shoved Trey to the side.

For a moment, he was confused, thinking she was pushing him away, then she was straddling him, riding him to a second, overwhelming wave of bliss.

She fell to the side and pulled him back over her, letting her fingers trail through his hair.

They were going as slowly as they could stand, stroke by agonizing stroke, deep kisses, and then Trey stopped abruptly.

Daniella opened the eyes she'd closed in ecstasy.

"I must not... too soon..." His face was tight with need and struggle.

Daniella made a little noise of delight. "I don't know what world you come from where making a woman come twice is too soon, but you've earned your turn..."

She arched up against him, grinding with her hips. He whimpered and began to thrust again, fast and desperate, and when his release washed over him, Daniella felt yet another wave of pleasure break over her as well.

They lay together in sweaty, panting bliss and Daniella let her hands trail over his chest, his taut stomach. He stroked her arms and shoulders, and kissed the top of her head.

"Merry Christmas," Trey told her solemnly.

Daniella could not help but giggle, feeling slightly high from the whole experience.

"Best Christmas present *ever*," she said.

Abruptly, he sat up. "I did not intend this as your present," he said, abashed. "I give you my glass prison, I give you myself. I pledge myself to your service, to your protection."

Daniella sat up with him, her knee knocking against his. "You don't have to…"

"I love you, Daniella. I have lost my entire world and all of my purpose, and then I look in your eyes and I feel like I have come home." He took her hands in his. "Let me stay with you. Let me learn how to court you in the ways of this place and earn a place at your side."

Overwhelmed, Daniella felt her eyes fill with tears. "Trey…"

"*Your* Trey, if you'll have me."

Daniella couldn't answer. She wanted to pledge herself to him, promise her heart, swear her love… but she didn't trust her voice… or her heart.

She could only pull him down on her again, and when he touched his lips to hers, she felt like a fire was lit there, a fire that went to the bottom of her soul and burned away every doubt and hesitation: a fire that could melt glass.

CHAPTER 13

They made love a second time later that night, and Trey had never known joy like falling asleep with Daniella cradled bonelessly in his arms.

He woke feeling deeply content, staring up at the ceiling and its fire-less lantern. It was cold and dark right now, but Daniella had shown him the switch on the wall that would bring it to life. The curtains over the window had been left askew, and there was light streaming in from the street lanterns outside.

There was so much in this world that was wonderful and full of beauty. Trey rose up on one elbow and gazed down at the woman lying beside him.

Her dark hair was splayed out over the pillow, and the lines of her face were soft in sleep.

She had no idea how amazing she was.

In his world, she would have been a sorceress of great power. Here, she considered herself a commoner, a simple person, every word she spoke denying how special she clearly was. She'd faced down dours without flinching, saved people without expecting recognition, and opened her home to him—a complete stranger, a foreign unknown!—without hesitation.

So brave. So beautiful.

And she was his.

Trey didn't understand his own certainty. Surely, she was out of his league, surely he was taking terrible liberties by pressing his suit upon her.

But he could not deny the connection he felt, or her return of the feelings that were overwhelming him.

Somehow, across worlds, this was the woman he was meant for. He saw it in her endless eyes, felt it in his chest. She completed him, fit him like the sheath to his lost sword.

Trey had never expected to feel peace; he had been trained for a desperate war from a young age and moments of joy were all he had ever been able to wish for.

But Daniella's slightest touch made happiness and hope feel like possibilities.

"Are you just going to stare at me, or are you going to kiss me?" While Trey had been gazing at her, Daniella's eyes had fluttered open, and her smile was slow and inviting.

Trey didn't need a second appeal, bending to enfold her in his arms and kiss her obediently.

He could have done more than worship her with his mouth, even on the heels of a night like they'd just shared, but Daniella pulled away after a deep, satisfying kiss.

"I have to let Fabio out," she said regretfully. "Do you want some breakfast?"

Trey's stomach grumbled at the idea, though there had been points the evening before where he was not sure it was physically possible to eat more food. "Surprisingly, yes," he observed.

"How do Christmas dinner leftovers sound?" Daniella offered as she dressed.

"Almost as delicious as you," Trey growled.

Daniella's sultry laugh made Trey reconsider breakfast compared to other options, but she was escaping out of the bedroom door to greet a frantic Fabio before he could recapture her and drag her back under the covers.

When she returned with Fabio and rush of cold air, Trey had reluctantly dressed himself and was cautiously opening cabinets in the kitchen. He felt brave enough to sort out plates and silverware, but was not foolish enough to attempt the refrigerator or the oven.

Daniella expressed her appreciation of even that feeble help, kissing him on the cheek as he helped her take off her coat. Fabio milled about, clearly excited by his journey outdoors and eager to say good morning to Trey.

"I was thinking that we might go to the second hand store and see about getting you a change of clothes," Daniella suggested. "It's not actually open, but I have a key. I'm supposed to get inventory done before New Year's, but I can set my own hours between now and then."

"You dictate *hours?*" Trey was cautiously awed. Could this world change the flux of time itself?

"Er, no," Daniella chuckled as she set down a hot plate of leftovers in front of him; she had a smaller cube of technology that would heat one plate at a time very quickly, which certainly *seemed* like it was changing time. "I get to choose which hours to *work*, which is itself a crazy luxury after the pre-Christmas madness of juggling double shifts at the cafe. You can start eating without me."

Trey reluctantly did, fearing disrespect despite her assurance. It was not as wildly delicious as it had been the night before and the portion was considerably smaller, but it was satisfying food and he was grateful for it. It wasn't long before Daniella was sitting opposite from him, eating from her own plate.

"Tell me more about your shieldmates," Daniella encouraged. "Had you trained together very long?"

The good food grew tasteless. "We were children together, raised to fight from the time we first manifested our gifts."

Daniella was not unaware of his discomfort, and hastened to fill the conversational space. "I grew up here in Wimberlette," she said softly. "People have moved in and out of town since I was a kid, but there are still a lot of familiar faces. A lot of the kids I went to school with have gone away to college, but some have gotten married, settled down, started families."

As Daniella had keyed into his own disquiet, Trey immediately picked up on hers. "You are sorry you didn't? Go to college"—a magical academy?—"or start a family?" The idea of her as a mother was both deeply disturbing and weirdly appealing.

Daniella's tanned skin colored and she focused on cutting her ham into unnecessarily small pieces. "That's… sort of what you're expected to do. But I didn't really have money or… college aspirations, and I didn't ever find anyone I wanted to start a family with."

A family.

Trey had learned about families. Mothers and husbands and children. Grandparents with gray hair, all together in a house to share duties and expenses. A bond of blood, nothing like the bond of oath he shared with his shieldmates and Robin.

He looked at the top of Daniella's head, considering.

Could they be a family?

For a moment he dared to hope. This world was quiet and peaceful, and he already loved her. Could they make a home together, could he settle here safely, find some meaningful work in her strange world of technology?

Then Daniella looked up and Trey knew that she was considering the same unexpected idea.

She put her fork down with a clatter. "We just met," she insisted, as if they had both been speaking out loud.

"You think it's too soon to think of a union," Trey said quietly. Now that he'd thought of it, he could think of nothing else. But she hadn't said that she loved him. Maybe she didn't. Trey knew that needs of the body were different than needs of the heart, even though he could no longer untangle the two when he looked at her.

They stared at one another helplessly until Daniella giggled. "Well, except for... you know... the kind of union we already had. I don't mind thinking about that..."

They both abandoned the few remains of their meal and met halfway over it, mouth against mouth.

Struggling against their clothing, they crashed through the tiny house to the bedroom again. Trey stripped her carefully and laid her down on the rumpled bed, licking her thighs and the round curves of her stomach before kissing his way up to her enchanting breasts and finally finding her mouth again.

"Oh, Trey," she breathed into his mouth. "You are my knight in shining armor."

"I have lost my armor," Trey protested. "And shining armor would not be particularly practical for stealth..."

"It's an expression," Daniella laughed. "I'll explain it... later."

Then she was wrapping her legs around him and Trey had no desire to speak of garments of war.

CHAPTER 14

Trey nearly froze and then scalded himself trying to master the shower controls while Daniella loaded the dishwasher, tidied up, and got out the vacuum. "We'll go to the second hand store and get you some more clothes after you… ah… wow."

Trey was standing in the doorway to the bathroom, as naked as the day he'd arrived, and he was holding a toilet plunger like a sword. Daniella realized that she had turned on the vacuum, and Trey was eyeing it with more distrust than even Fabio, who had gone to hide in the bedroom the moment she'd taken it from the closet.

Daniella turned it off. "It's a vacuum cleaner," she explained. "It sucks dirt and dog fur and pine needles off the floor. Real Christmas trees and real dogs come with downsides."

Trey lowered the toilet plunger. "Very well," he said, scowling at the thing suspiciously. "It sounds… useful."

Daniella gladly watched him turn around and return to the bathroom, then grinned and resumed her task, humming as she pushed the vacuum around underneath the shedding tree and skirted the couch. She was winding up the cord when Trey emerged from the bathroom again. He was dressed this time, and Daniella tried not to feel disappointed.

She dismantled the vacuum cleaner, just to show him how it worked, and felt like a salesman as she explained the attachments and various functions.

"It's wondrous," Trey said raptly, peering down one of the tubes.

Fabio, far less impressed, remained in the bedroom until the monstrosity had been replaced in the closet, then crept out and demanded pets and treats to atone for his time of torture.

"Peace, fair hound," Trey told him, stroking his ears and feeding him entirely too many treats from the box. "Your alarm is very understandable."

Daniella watched them with a foolish smile on her face that faded as she thought achingly that this was everything she'd ever wanted. Almost everything. She remembered his pledge to her. Was that just a matter of honor? Or was it something more?

When Trey looked up at her with a broad grin showing his straight, white teeth, she couldn't help but smile again in return.

"Would you… would you be willing to change for me again?"

Trey's face went confused.

Daniella went shyly on. "To a dragon, I mean. You were beautiful, and… I know you weren't as large as you expected, but you were still pretty amazing."

Trey stood, and his expressive face betrayed the conflict he was feeling: pride, shame, and longing, all mixed up.

Then, without speaking, he shimmered and shrank,

and he was again the most astonishing creature that Daniella had ever seen.

She knew what to expect this time, and Fabio only barked once before coming bravely forward to sniff at the knee-high dragon. Daniella cocked her head at it. Was he a little larger than last time? Maybe it only looked that way in the small room. He certainly was still no danger to her house. She knelt to touch him, and his scales were smooth and silky under her fingers.

Trey hissed a gentle warning to Fabio when his sniffing got enthusiastic, then put his front claws up on Daniella's knees. She opened her arms, and he swarmed up onto her.

Lighter than she expected, he twined up onto her shoulder, using his long tail for balance, slipped under her ponytail, and rubbed a knobby head behind her opposite ear. His wings were folded tight up against his body, and his claws were careful, just gripping her without causing pain. The claws didn't appear to be retractable, like a cat's, but he could lift them away and use the pads of his forefeet like fingertips.

He was green and, up close, his scales gleamed like gemstones, with hidden, glittery depths teasing at the edges of Daniella's vision. She stroked his tail and he made a happy rumbling sound like a purr.

Fabio whined and tried to jump up, clearly jealous that Trey got to scale his mistress, while he was bound to the ground.

"No jumping," Daniella said breathlessly to the dog. It was magical, having a lithe little dragon on her shoulder. Fabio sulked.

Trey walked out on her arm when she held it up in front of her, and spread out his breathtaking wings. They were mottled green, with that same jewel-like depth that his scales had, and semi-transparent like bat wings. He dipped his head, and Daniella wondered if he didn't look a little abashed.

"You aren't too small," Daniella assured him. "You're *personal-sized*. It is perfect. I have always wanted a dragon I could cuddle."

He rolled glittering eyes at her, then fell from her arm, spreading wings to glide above the floor and sweep into the air.

It was a temptation that Fabio could not resist, and he barked and chased, colliding into the Christmas tree as Trey banked around it.

For one breathless moment, Daniella was sure that disaster was imminent, and she wondered in panic what would happen if Trey's glass dragon was broken. Then he was standing as a man again, catching the tree as it started to topple and Fabio crashed into his legs.

Trey took the full force of the dog's momentum, bending his knees to absorb the impact. The tree flexed in his grip, and the lights danced as the tinsel fell in all directions.

His ornament, heavy and fragile, slipped from its jostled branch and Daniella gave a small sound of horror as it fell.

Trey twisted, impossibly fast, reached out, and caught it just before it hit the floor.

Everyone was still for a heartbeat, even Fabio.

"If you hadn't caught it," Daniella said breathlessly. "Would you...?"

Trey straightened back up, the ornament held carefully in his hands. "I am still connected to it in some way," he said gravely. "I suspect it is my only chance to return to my own world."

Daniella felt her heart seize in her chest at the idea of Trey leaving her to go back to the place he'd come from.

*D*aniella's sudden distance did not go unnoticed. Something had bothered her, but Trey wasn't sure what. Fabio demanded reassurance at his mistress' hand, and she knelt and hugged him tight.

She had definitely been frightened by the near-fall of the ornament, but Trey wondered if it wasn't something more. Should he offer her comfort? She'd been so delighted by his dragon form…

Without thinking twice, he hung the ornament back on the tree and shifted. He came to worm his way in with Fabio, until she had an armful of both dragon and dog and she was laughing again in relief and delight.

Fabio, abashed by his embarrassing crash, tried to lick him, but was gentle about it, and his tail wagged slowly.

Daniella stood with Trey cradled in her arms, gave Fabio a pat on the head, and retreated to the couch, where she curled up with the dragon.

"You're less… spiky than I thought you'd be," she observed, stroking his wings and trailing her fingers down his tail.

It wasn't as erotic being under her fingers as it was when he was in human form, but it was comforting; Trey could see why Fabio liked being petted so much. His eyes closed, and he found himself humming in pleasure.

When he shifted again, he was lying with his head in Daniella's lap, and it seemed like the perfect place to be.

CHAPTER 15

Daniella was beginning to understand that there were topics that should be avoided. Childhood. His shieldmates, who were clearly badly missed. His world. Their future.

But there was plenty that they could discuss. Sex. Fabio. Television. Technology; Trey was wildly curious about so many things that Daniella had always taken for granted. She even dug out some pre-college textbooks that she'd gotten when her ambitions were higher and they pored over math and history and English, just to find baselines with each other.

In general, he was so smart, and oh, so sexy... "Oh, yeah, that looks *great*."

He was plucking at the shirt curiously, standing outside the curtained corner that served as a dressing room at the second hand store.

"I confess, I did not believe it would fit, but the fabric... it is remarkably *stretchy*."

He was wearing a black t-shirt emblazoned with a car

logo, and it was *extremely* stretchy over his mounds of muscles.

Daniella licked her lips. She would not have guessed that after the night they'd just had… and the morning before they left… that she would have these kinds of stirrings again for a good long time. But Trey, flexing in front of the mirror, would have raised her interest from the absolute dead. "We'll get that one."

"As you wish," he agreed.

"Try this on," Daniella suggested, holding up a collared shirt.

Trey stripped out of the t-shirt and Daniella momentarily lost her power of speech.

When he frowned over the buttons, she stepped forward to help him, and she breathed in the dizzying musky scent of him. "I, er, yes, this one will do, too. Yup."

It wasn't a perfect fit—just a little short in the sleeves—but it buttoned, at least, and it only had a small stain at the hem. It was also only a dollar.

"Should we be selecting clothing for you as well?" Trey asked, fingering someone's abandoned prom dress. "It seems unfair that only I'm being attired."

Daniella could have pointed out that she had an entire closet filled with clothing already, as compared to Trey, who had come to their world completely—gloriously!—naked. But he was looking at her with hot, dark eyes, and she realized that other than her cafe uniform, he'd only seen her in jeans and t-shirts. Maybe it *was* unfair…

"I'll try that on, if you try these on," she agreed, holding up a pair of leather pants that she strongly doubted that Trey would fit into. It would at least be fun to watch him try.

"You drive a hard bargain," he teased her, eyes twinkling. "I agree to your terms."

Daniella shot a look at the cameras in the corners of the warehouse. Ansel had explained that they were only for show, not actually connected to a security system; the blinking red light was battery powered and they did nothing else.

She shucked off her shirt, flattered by Trey's avid attention, and unbuttoned her pants, then slowly pulled them off. The effect was ruined by losing her balance while her legs were still tangled in her jeans, and she gave a graceless squawk and nearly fell on her ass. Trey, laughing, caught her, and if his hands weren't entirely chaste while he set her back onto her feet, Daniella had no complaints.

He helped her pull the shimmery prom dress over her head and smooth it into place.

It was a perfect fit, to Daniella's surprise, leaving an amount of cleavage that would have sent her own high school prom chaperons into fits and showing a long length of leg on one side. The silk (probably not real silk, with a $15 price tag) was a mottled blue and green, possibly hand-dyed. The puffed sleeves were straight out of a fairy tale and it was trimmed generously with silver brocade.

"You are magnificent," Trey observed without the slightest touch of mockery.

Daniella crossed her arms over her overflowing breasts self-consciously. "I believe this was part of an arrangement," she reminded him.

The pants she'd found were indeed at least two sizes too small for Trey's muscular legs, but he gave it a game try, pulling and stretching and squeezing for Daniella's entertainment. It was every bit as much fun as she had suspected it would be and he hammed it up delightfully, making sure to turn and give her the best view possible as he tugged at the protesting waistband.

"I concede," he laughed. "They have won!"

"Oh no," Daniella laughed, "I am definitely the one who won here." She gave a golf clap that made her cleavage bounce in a way guaranteed to pull his attention, though he was trying gamely not to stare. "We'll buy those, for sure."

He looked puzzled. "But they do not fit."

"They don't have to. I'm buying them to watch you try to put them on again."

They laughed together as they continued trading clothing to try on. Trey convinced Daniella to buy the blue silk dress though she had no earthly purpose for a prom dress, and she found a pair of jeans tight enough to show off every line of his beautiful legs. They found more ridiculous costumes to try on: a clown wig and a ridiculous fur coat, paisley leggings and ugly plaid overalls, a cowboy hat and a pair of assless chaps, a dress covered with dinosaurs that barely covered Daniella's underwear. They marched the aisles in platform shoes and flip flops, trailing superhero capes and brandishing wooden swords, and Daniella showed him the holiday-themed shelf where she'd found his glass ornament.

The sound of their mirth echoed through the warehouse, and neither of them noticed the small dark shape, like a cat but not, that scurried from a shadowed corner and slithered out into the snow.

CHAPTER 16

Trey, having successfully persuaded Daniella to purchase the dress that made her look like royalty, agreed to a pile of clothing that exceeded Trey's prior garment allowance. She solemnly answered his concerned questions about currency, and showed him the paper and coins that served as tender for trade.

"I will need to compensate you," Trey said thoughtfully. "Perhaps there is some labor I could find payment for?"

"We'll work something out," Daniella said, with a cautious sideways look. She was always careful about talking about the future with him.

She took him to her other place of employment, an eating establishment called "Marie's."

"Anna's already seen you," Daniella said with resignation as they entered and found a free table to sit at. She gave a friendly wave to the woman wearing a uniform. "So there's no point in trying to keep you a secret. Probably the entire town knows about you now. If anyone asks, you're from Norway. That will cover your accent and odd manners."

"From Norway," Trey agreed. "I am Norwaydian."

"Norwegian," Daniella corrected.

"Nor-WEE-gian," Trey copied her. "And we met on a dating site."

"Tinder," Daniella said. "That's believable."

"A fire was lit," Trey said with approval.

"Was it ever," Daniella laughed helplessly. He was holding her hand across the table.

"Can I get you guys something to drink?" the uniformed attendant asked. She was carrying a steaming pitcher of a liquid as dark as her skin and grinning. "Coffee?"

Trey gave Daniella a swift look for direction and she nodded. "Two coffees, please."

The server filled white cups that were already laid out on the table.

"I am Nor-WEE-gian," Trey volunteered. "We met on a dating site. Kindling."

"Tinder," Daniella wheezed weakly, clearly trying not to laugh.

"Ah… okay, I'm Leann." The woman glanced at Daniella. "You've been holding out on me, hon."

"This is Trey," Daniella introduced.

"Are you planning to stay in Wimberlette long?" Leann asked, completely innocently.

The tension that settled over the table was palpable.

"Until my business has concluded," Trey decided it was safe to say, just as Daniella said, "A couple of weeks, maybe."

Leann nodded knowingly. "I'll give you guys a few minutes to look over the menu. Dinner's available, but we have breakfast all day." She bustled off to refill coffees at other tables; the establishment was about half full, and Trey was aware that he and Daniella were the object of many curious glances and hushed, smiling conversations.

A new woman came to take their order once Daniella had quietly explained the menu and the ordering process to him. "I'm Marie," she introduced herself to Trey. "Daniella hasn't told us anything about you."

Trey recognizing her name from the identification on the building. "You have a lovely establishment," he praised her. "It smells delightful."

"He's from Norway," Daniella was quick to explain. "We... ah, met on Tinder."

"So Leann said," Marie said with a grin. "Well, a *friend* of Daniella's is a friend of ours. Welcome to Wimberlette."

"Thank you," Trey said gravely.

"Have you decided on your food or do you need a little longer?"

"Cinnamon French Toast meal for me," Daniella selected. "With bacon and hashfries."

"Daniella recommends the chicken fried steak, with hash browns," Trey said trustingly. "She assures me that all of your food is most excellent."

"Good choice," Marie said approvingly. She winked at Trey and swept away.

"I... er... hope that I am not besmirching your reputation," Trey said in a whisper over the table.

Daniella whispered back, "Are you kidding? You are *making* my reputation. I got myself a hotty from Europe. Every single woman here is going to sign up for Tinder and start searching for Norwaydian hunks."

While they waited for their food service, Daniella quietly pointed out their service ware and explained the various condiments on the table. Trey tasted the red sauce she warned was hot.

"That is a sauce worthy of a dragon," he said approvingly. Then he thought to ask, "Do you have shifters of any kind here?"

Daniella looked thoughtfully back. "We have stories, about werewolves and other cryptids, but they are only accepted as mythology. If they exist, they are quiet and hidden."

Trey nodded thoughtfully. "There tends to be truth in stories when they are told often enough, but I can see why they would be shy in this world."

"Cinnamon French Toast," Marie announced, placing a plate before Daniella.

Daniella sat up and pulled a paper napkin into her lap. Trey copied her as Marie put a steaming platter smothered in a lumpy white gravy in front of him. A sidelong look through the room reinforced his impression that Marie was not waiting on anyone else in the eatery. Daniella must be a person of importance in these parts.

"My thanks," he said gravely.

"You folks need anything else?" Marie asked.

"We're good," Daniella said easily. "It all looks great."

Trey duplicated Daniella's manners, taking a bite of the food on his plate. "This does not taste like chicken," he said approvingly.

"It's… er, not?" Daniella laughed through a mouthful of her rather more attractive meal. "Chicken-fried refers to the breading and the way the steak is cooked."

"It does not taste like bread, either," Trey observed. The gravy was familiar—a creamy, thick, flavorful sauce with chunks of sausage. The meat beneath was tender and strong, with a strangely crispy shell. The potato shreds were also unexpectedly crunchy and enjoyable. The spicy red sauce took it all up to the next level of delicious, and Trey devoured his plate of food eagerly.

He also had Daniella's last bites, savoring the sweet spiced flavor of her fried pastry.

"Your world has many advantages," he said to her frankly, glad that he had not put on the tighter of the pants she had insisted he buy.

Daniella glanced around at his slip but seemed satisfied that no one was in earshot. "You mean like it hasn't been taken over by evil black smoke that makes everyone angry?"

She looked like she regretted the words, but Trey answered firmly, "That is primary among its qualities, yes. And on my word, I will find a way to keep it that way."

Her brown eyes softened. "You are pretty amazing, you know?"

"Who's taking the check?" Leann asked. Marie had apparently conceded her service of their table, her curiosity satisfied for the time.

"Oh, that's me," Daniella said quickly. "Overseas credit cards, you know. Don't always work."

Leann looked puzzled. "Well, we don't get a *lot* of visitors, but we haven't had any trouble with foreign cards."

Daniella blushed. "Ah, well, sure…"

"My currency is different," Trey intervened, remembering Daniella's lessons about their money, which had involved talking briefly about other countries. "I must have some converted."

"You're going to have trouble finding a bank in Wimberlette that will take crowns," Leann observed, and Trey and Daniella both looked at her blankly until she explained, "You know, Norwegian crowns."

"Right," Daniella said with a jolt of understanding. "Right. That's going to be hard. We might have to drive to Grand Rapids."

Trey suspected they were not talking about head adornments of royalty.

Daniella laughed nervously. "Ah, anyway, here's my card. My treat. Oh, We really ought to get home to let Fabio out."

She signed the paper that Leann brought her and left a few pieces of her paper money on the table in addition, and they went back out into the snow.

"Well," Daniella said in relief, "I guess that went better than my last time at the cafe."

The last time, there had been dours at the cafe, Trey remembered abruptly. He frowned, remembering his promise to protect the world. He wished Robin would return; he had so many questions.

CHAPTER 17

They walked home to release an ecstatic Fabio from Daniella's house and decided to take him down to the park to work off some of their fullness.

Daniella tucked her arm easily into Trey's elbow, and they walked closely, perfectly in stride.

There were kids out, having impromptu snowball fights and playing complicated games that involved chasing and yelling over the playground equipment. Fabio strained at the end of his leash, wanting to join them, but Daniella scratched his ears and kept him close. He sighed and sulked.

"What are these things?" Trey asked.

Daniella looked up from her attention to Fabio. "Swings!" she said. "Want me to push you?"

"I am not certain," Trey said dubiously.

"C'mon," Daniella coaxed. "I'll show you."

She looped Fabio's leash around one of the posts and got Trey seated on the tallest of the swings. It was still short for his long legs, and he dragged his feet in the snow until he got the knack of tucking them up underneath him as Daniella called out how to coordinate his weight and legs with the back and forth swing as she struggled to push him.

"You're ginormous," she complained good-naturedly, slipping in the slushy snow.

"If I continue to eat your chicken-steaks, I will undoubtedly collapse your puny swings," Trey laughed in return.

Daniella gave him another Herculean push and nearly ended on her backside. He had the idea of *pumping* well in hand now, so she scrambled to take the swing next to him, scooching back as far as she could manage on her feet and then kicking her legs out.

They competed for height, laughing and straining against the cold metal chains, and Daniella caught herself singing in sheer joy.

As soon as she realized it, she stopped herself.

"Don't stop," Trey said, as they both slowed. "Your voice is like… fruitcake."

Daniella smiled despite herself. "Fruitcake?"

"Beautiful and full of light."

"But it tastes terrible?"

Trey reached out and caught the chain of her swing. "You taste amazing," he said, lowering his mouth to hers. When he released her from the kiss, a cluster of nearby children loudly protested.

"Gross!" "Ew!" There was a lot of giggling and they took their play across to the merry go round on the other end of the park. Fabio strained at the end of his leash, whining and wagging his tail.

"We're scandalizing the locals," Daniella said, kissing him again.

Trey drew back a moment, trying to decide if she was

serious, then kissed her soundly back. "Let them be scandalized," he said firmly.

When they let go of each other, they swung back into place and traced their feet in snow. He wasn't that much older than she was, Daniella realized. He was so built and full of confidence that he seemed much older, but he didn't have much stubble after a few days without shaving, and every so often, his glance was uncertain and adorable.

She thought about having to be a warrior so young, in a world without hope.

"Why do you stop?" he asked.

"Stop what?" Daniella looked up and met his eyes.

"You start to sing and then you stop yourself. You do it a lot."

His eyes... Daniella had never seen eyes like them before. They were so complicated and entrancing, and green just like the glass he'd come from. She hadn't even realized that she'd started singing, let alone that she'd stopped. "I... oh, I used to sing a lot."

"But you don't now?"

Daniella laughed sheepishly. "No," she said shortly. She ducked her head in embarrassment. Everyone local knew her story, but she found that she didn't want to admit it to Trey.

"I don't want to pry," Trey said, in that tone that really meant he wanted to.

"I used to sing a lot," Daniella explained. "I was in all the school talent shows, used to bust out in show tunes all the time, sing karaoke."

Trey blinked at her and she realized that she was going to have to simplify her explanation. "I sang a *lot*, and there was... this contest."

She was twisting in the swing, dragging one foot through the pea gravel beneath her. Most of the snow was gone beneath them now, kicked away to the gravel beneath.

Daniella continued sheepishly. "There was this thing, this contest, in Milwaukee, on television, and the whole town got together to send me down to it. Everyone was sure I could win it."

"You didn't," Trey guessed.

Daniella shook her head. "Didn't even place." She pursed her lips. "I was a small fish in a smaller town, and there were singers that didn't make finals that wiped the floor with me. It was… really humiliating. No one asks me to sing for anything now."

"Because you feel so bad about it?" Trey suggested.

"Because…" Daniella hesitated. She'd spent a long time telling herself that they didn't want her singing because they were disappointed in her… but she wondered how much of it was that everyone knew how ashamed she felt, and they didn't want her to feel bad. No one had ever been the slightest bit unkind about it.

"I was in a contest once," Trey said gently. "Well, lots of contests, and most of them I won. But it's easier to remember the ones I lost."

Daniella didn't think he was trying to brag, only explain, and she let him go on without judgment.

"There was an important one, when I was young. One I should have won, and didn't. I felt terrible for it, carried it around like a weight, trained harder. And a year later, I swore I would win it… and when I told my shieldmates my fears that I wouldn't succeed, they didn't even remember that I hadn't. They only remembered their own failures, their own embarrassments."

Trey reached over and gathered one of her hands up in both of his. "You have a beautiful gift of a voice, and you should share it. No one carries your failures like you do yourself."

Daniella's throat felt very tight and uncomfortable. "You're right," she whispered. "Dammit."

Fabio, fearing that there was attention he wasn't getting, came to the end of his leash and touched her knee with his nose.

"Will you sing for me, sometimes?" Trey asked.

"Yeah," Daniella said, blushing. "I'd like that."

"Now?" Trey said hopefully.

"I can't think of anything to sing," she laughed. It was true. Given the opportunity, she could not think of anything she felt confident enough to sing. It had been so long since someone had asked her to.

"Christmas songs?"

"Oh no," Daniella said in horror. "Singing Christmas songs after Christmas is a terrible offense."

She could watch Trey file that away as valuable information and wondered if she hadn't overplayed it a touch.

She looked beyond him. "I think those kids want to use this swings," she said, standing. Trey bowed formally to the children and took Fabio's leash from the post as Daniella re-wrapped the scarf that had come loose around her neck while she was swinging.

He looked back over his shoulder at them wistfully. "It's a joy to see that," he said, as he pulled Daniella's arm back into his elbow. "They are so... unafraid."

"You didn't get much of a childhood, did you," Daniella observed.

"That is... not what I would call it," he said sorrowfully. Behind them, the kids were laughing and negotiating who would push, voices loud and fearless.

Daniella suddenly remembered the dours, and the faces of her friends under their influence and shuddered to think about that kind of hatred creeping over their innocent features. Trey put his arm around her. Daniella wasn't sure if he knew why she had shivered, or if he only thought to keep her warm, but she leaned into his comforting strength gratefully.

CHAPTER 18

Trey fell into a comfortable pattern with Daniella, a familiar routine that satisfied his need for structure. They made love at night, again in the morning, and sometimes in the afternoon, when he couldn't resist the laughing sidelong glances she gave him.

She taught him to navigate her miraculous kitchen, and he was relieved to find that the bottle in the fridge was a fruit paste called ketchup, not a vessel of blood, as he'd first assumed. Near the end of the week, he was able to make them a few meals, and feed himself when she went to work.

On the last day of the week, they slept late. Trey was used to a strict wake-up schedule, but it was so blissful waking up with Daniella tangled in the luxurious bedding with him that he sometimes dozed longer.

Daniella rolled to look at the glowing numbers on the bedside clock.

"Oh crap," she said. "I've got to finish inventory and there's a *lot* still to do." She rolled back onto her back rather than hurrying away. "It probably won't matter much because it's not open to customers, but Ansel wants inventory done before year's end so he can get taxes done right away."

"When does the year end?" Trey asked, pulling her into his arms for kisses and meeting no resistance.

"Tonight," Daniella whispered.

"Can it wait an hour or two?" Trey suggested, finding the sensitive place along her hip that had given her such delight the night before.

"I really should go in…" Daniella moaned. But she kissed him back, and it was another hour before she showered and finally left.

Trey later wandered out of the bathing chamber wrapped in a towel and sat for a time petting Fabio and reading the fairy tale book that Daniella had given him. It had illustrations of dragons.

"We've got trouble," Robin said, popping through a portal near his shoulder.

Fabio gave a yelp of surprise at the fable's appearance, then attempted to climb onto the back of the couch to lick them.

Trey, with plenty of practice now, grabbed him by the collar and dragged him gently back. "What trouble do you speak of, Robin?"

"Daniella is in danger," Robin said, alighting on the back of the couch.

Trey was in motion at once, throwing off the towel and hurrying to get dressed. "Tell me!" he demanded. "I need a blacksmith. Armor. A sword. I have to protect her."

"You're going to have a lot of trouble finding that here," Robin warned him. "They fight very differently."

"As a dragon, then," Trey said firmly. Then he remembered that his magic form was diminutive like Robin in this world. "Tell me what's happening."

"Remember how I said the veil between worlds had gotten thin? It turns out that it's a cyclical thing. At the end of every calendar year, the veil gets thinner and thinner, then it resets at the turn of the year. I'm sure it's no coincidence that this world has such a calendar. This is the last day of the year, this is the weakest point. Cerad is going to make his move tonight."

"Where will he be? Where will they come through?"

"Where we first came through," Robin said miserably. "The warehouse where Daniella found you."

"Where she is working now," Trey realized with horror, halfway into his jeans.

"There's more," Robin cautioned.

"There always is," Trey said bitterly, jerking his shirt over his head.

"Daniella is your key."

There was a thread in Robin's voice that arrested Trey. "What does that mean?"

"It wasn't chance that she found you, or that she broke the spell. Daniella is your...counterpart in this world, your anchor here. The deeper and truer your connection, the stronger you will be here."

"I...I love her," Trey confessed.

"I hope that will be enough," Robin said grimly. "When I went searching for Henrik, I found only his key, in a place called South Carolina. I think she can help us, even if we do not have our shieldmate with us yet."

"I have to protect Daniella," Trey said firmly as he pulled on the last of his clothing. "How do I get to her?" Fabio got excited at the sound of his mistress' name and came to the door with him.

"She's *your* key," Robin said helplessly. "How would I know?"

"The warehouse..." Daniella had driven him there, and

Trey was not familiar with the landmarks of the town yet. Fabio was getting excited and his tail was wagging furiously as he attempted to stay between Trey and the door.

When Trey opened the door, not really sure where he was going, but sure that he had to try, Fabio bolted out. He ran as far as the sidewalk, then turned and looked back expectantly. "Can you take me to Daniella, hound?" Trey asked hopefully. "Daniella?"

Fabio looked at him vacantly, his feathered tail sweeping back and forth.

Just as Trey was deciding that the canine would be of no use, Fabio's tail stilled and his head swiveled.

Trey, looking that direction, felt his heart drop. He didn't have to wonder where Daniella was…there was an unnatural black fog creeping over the far side of the town. He knew that he had only to follow that darkness to find his love. He crouched, and then leaped into the air, shifting as he went, and he was astonished to find that he was his full, glorious size again.

Beneath him, Fabio howled in outrage at his abandonment and then began to run after him.

CHAPTER 19

Daniella smiled as she trailed her hand over the shelf she'd found Trey on, bemused by the warmth in her chest from the memory.

So many memories.

His expression when faced with the refrigerator. The way he'd knelt and pledged himself to her. His kiss. His big hands on...

Daniella cleared her throat loudly in the echoing, empty shop and ducked her head even though no one was there to notice her blush.

She was being absolutely ridiculous. She was acting like a fool over some guy that she'd known for less than a week. She was...

Daniella paused, one hand on her clipboard, one on the pile of neatly folded men's pants.

She was *in love* with him.

It was utterly absurd. He was a gorgeous man from another world, and he'd wanted her, and she was so desperate to be wanted that she was spinning a *relationship* out of a couple of hot nights of sex. And a few hot mornings. And a lot of hungry kisses at lots of other times.

Daniella realized she was smiling foolishly when she caught sight of her reflection in a mirror, then frowned and turned.

Nothing was there.

The skittering shadow she'd seen must have just been a trick of the light, just a mistaken glance through the distortion of the mirror.

Daniella moved on to T-shirts and started counting again.

She made it halfway down that aisle, more slowly than she usually worked because she kept losing count as she remembered how Trey had looked when he tasted fruitcake, and the way it felt when he was bending to kiss her and his hair fell around her.

She shook her head, jotting down a number on the pad that would be close enough. "I have got to get it together," she scolded herself.

And this time, she was looking straight at the shadow when it moved.

It was understandable that she had mistaken it for a cat, the first time. It was about the size of a cat, and close to the ground. It even had the silky grace of a cat. But it had too many limbs to be a cat, and then no limbs at all, and it twisted impossibly and moved more like a wisp of smoke than a walking beast.

It detached from behind the end of the shelf and drifted *towards* her.

"Oh, you've got to be kidding me," Daniella said.

It paused when she spoke, and shivered.

"You can't hurt me," she told it, and she was reassured by the fact that it stopped, swirling thoughtfully in place at the sound of her voice.

It was speaking that had stopped the last ones, she realized. Each time, she had said something out loud, and they had fled their victims.

This one wasn't fleeing, and it started towards her again, though its approach now was distinctly reluctant.

A second form detached itself from the shadows near the bottom of the shelves, and then a third, each of them slinking towards Daniella.

"I know what you are now," she said firmly, backing into the shelf behind her. A line from *Labyrinth* occurred to her. "You have no power over me!"

But there were more shadows now, spilling over the shelves and around them, dozens of them.

"You can't hurt me!" she cried, and they all paused and shivered in place, but started forward again as soon as her voice stopped.

Daniella scurried back down the aisle away from them and drew up at the end of the shelves. There were more of the dours coming from every direction. Hundreds of them, making the far end of the warehouse look like it was full of dark fog.

"You can't hurt me!" she repeated fiercely. "All you can do is make me afraid, and angry, and I know what you are, and you can't stop me now."

They slowed at her voice, but continued coming, crowding closer, and closer as Daniella kept talking, as loudly and continuously as she could. "If Fabio were here, you'd be scattering to the winds," she said scornfully. "He'd... well, he'd probably try to lick you. And dog spit, man, that's nothing to play around with. You'd be sorry you ever messed around with us, you know."

They swirled away and oozed forward again, like the cold mist that crept inside on really cold days, almost as if they were being pushed towards her by the sheer mass of the ones behind them.

"My boyfriend is a scary fae dragon shifter!" Daniella blustered. A cat-sized dragon, she didn't mention. "He's not going to be amused by you harassing me."

Daniella nearly tripped over a step stool, and then climbed up on top of it as if they were mice... as if being two feet taller was going to stop them from suffocating her simply with their abundance.

"You can't hurt me!" Daniella protested, knowing she sounded desperate. "You're only fear and I won't let you rule me!"

They milled around beneath her feet, not offering to climb up on her.

Then there was something else in the darkness at the end of the building, something that walked fearlessly from the squirming masses of the dours.

At first, Daniella questioned her vision, because her eyes simply refused to focus on the figure. But as it drew closer, and her stomach fell to somewhere near her knees, she realized it was wriggling, like the dours themselves. It was a squirming, blurry, not-quite-there shape, the height of Trey, but gaunt and shivery.

"We're not open to the public," Daniella told it firmly. She continued to babble, "I'm only doing inventory. By myself." That didn't help her feel any better at *all*, and while the thing seemed to flinch a little at the sound of her voice, it didn't seem as if she was able to push it back like she could with the dours.

The dours around his feet cowered back briefly at her words, but surged forward with every step the strange fluttery man took, swirling around his feet like dogs at the feet of hunting horses.

"You can't hurt me," Daniella said breathlessly.

"They can't hurt you," the creature hissed at her, his voice like frost in the air, "but I can!" From thin air, it pulled a long, black sword. "You are the key, and I am here to kill you before you ruin our plans."

It was at the end of the aisle now, and Daniella could look right into its skeletal gray face. Where there ought to be eyes were only dark pits, with swirling black fog filling them.

She stepped backwards, forgetting she was on the step stool, and nearly fell into the soup of dours beneath her. As she caught her balance, she cast about for something—anything!—she could use as a weapon. Across the aisle was home furnishings, and among the piles of old curtains and dish towels was a long, brass curtain rod. It was also... across the aisle.

Daniella glanced at the new horror, coming unhurried towards her, and back across the aisle and down at the teeming dours.

"You can't hurt me," she whispered, and then she was holding her breath as if she were stepping off of a diving board, and dropping into the dours.

It was like stepping into cold water and she was immediately numb to her knees. But Daniella could still force herself to move forward, and then the curtain rod was a comfortable weight in her hands as she ripped it off the shelf and turned.

She swung it down through the dours and it parted them briefly, like waving a hand through thick smoke.

There was a terrible sound that it took Daniella a moment to identify as a laugh—an awful, gleeful, humorless laugh. She looked up at the thing still gliding towards her and the curtain rod felt much less useful when he swung the sword at a shelf and sliced through it as if it were made of butter.

The shelf collapsed, spilling folded clothing and worthless baubles out into the aisle with a crash.

This would be a good time to run, Daniella told herself, and then she was sprinting away with terror giving her feet extra swiftness.

For a blissful moment, she thought she was going to escape; the door wasn't that far away, and the dours she was wading through barely slowed her.

Then there was a crackling sound and a dark tear before her, and the gaunt figure was stepping out of a big, black version of the sparkly little portal the fairy—fable—had used to teleport... right in front of her.

Daniella had too much momentum to stop herself, and she barreled directly into the creature, her curtain rod not very usefully at her side.

If it had taken the time to raise its sword, Daniella was quite certain that would have been the end of her. Instead, it was as surprised as she was, and they simply slammed ineffectively into each other.

Daniella dropped her curtain rod and watched in horror as the bleak raised its sword. She scrambled backwards, helpless and unarmed, as it stepped forward.

That was when the dragon came crashing through the ceiling.

And it was definitely no longer the size of a cat.

CHAPTER 20

Trey recognized the second-hand warehouse from above and circled it twice, trying to determine a way in.

Then he seemed to feel Daniella's despair rise up like a great wave and he made his own way in, folding his wings and diving at the roof.

Sheet metal ripped apart under his claws and wood beneath it splintered. As he peeled away the layers of the roof, scraps of insulation like goose down flying away from his savage attack, he could see Daniella standing below.

She and the bleak both looked up at his noisy entrance, and Trey saw that she was helpless against the bleak's advance. He folded his wings against his side and wriggled in through the hole in the roof, roaring his outrage.

The bleak raised his sword and charged Daniella, who sensibly turned and fled the length of the warehouse. She zig-zagged down the aisles as Trey glided overhead, trying to find a place to turn and dart down between them. There was just enough space above the shelves for brief flight, but he swiftly realized that he was better served hopping from shelf to shelf, not caring if they toppled behind him as he kicked off.

When he finally dropped between Daniella and the bleak, he was dismayed that the creature did not stand and fight, but slithered away behind him again; clearly the bleak's focus was the woman, not Trey.

Trey remembered Robin's words. Daniella was the key to Trey's power in this world. And Trey was the key to stopping Cerad from invading this world.

He was still not yet at his full strength; when he shot a jet of his light at the bleak, it flinched, but his fire did not appear to damage the creature or stop it from raising its sword to strike at Daniella where she stood, defenseless.

Trey leaped and streaked down at it, forcing it away from Daniella again with a shriek of rage as bits of the ceiling rained down around him. Nothing mattered but protecting her. Rows of heavy shelving rocked in place as he impacted the place the bleak had been standing. He folded his wings tight against his sides.

He struck at the bleak with outstretched claws, and whipped his tail around behind it.

It slithered into mist, unharmed, but it took a moment for it to reassemble, and those were moments when it couldn't hurt Daniella.

"Your shieldmates are shattered," the bleak hissed at him. "You're alone in this world, and are not enough to protect it from us."

Trey pounced forward, ignoring its dire words about his shieldmates, snarling. He managed to rend it into smoke once more. This time, it got a slash of its sword in before it dissolved, and Trey felt a line of heat along his scales. He didn't have time to inspect the injury; the bleak resumed its form swiftly, trying to get behind Trey to Daniella once more.

If it killed Daniella, Trey's power here would be severed, he realized, after several exchanges, knocking over heavy shelves and smashing a hole directly in the side of the building. His vow to save her world would be worthless if he couldn't also save her.

They raged up and down the building, the bleak drawing thin lines of blood along Trey's sides as they battled. Daniella drew down beneath the sales counter where she had the most protection.

A bark distracted Trey for a moment, allowing the bleak to stab into one of his clawed feet, and Trey gave a howl of pain that was echoed by Fabio's howl as the hound wormed his way in through the hole that Trey had punched in the wall. He must have followed Trey on four paws.

Trey curled his claws painfully around the sword that was sticking through his foot and attempted to wrest it from the bleak, rising on his hind legs to swipe with his free claws. For a moment, he thought that he would disarm his enemy, but the bleak pulled the sword back at the last moment, leaving his whole limb burning in agony.

Trey flamed and gave a limping charge forward, a charge he aborted at the last moment because Fabio was somehow before the bleak, growling and snarling in canine challenge.

"Fabio! Fabio, come!!" Daniella was standing again, trying to coax her hound away from the battle.

Trey couldn't speak in dragon form, but he gave a rumble of frustration and changed directions at the last moment, staggering heavily into one of the fallen shelves and tripping over a tangled rack of hanging clothes as he tried to put weight on his injured limb.

The bleak laughed, a sound that made Fabio whine and flinch away, as Trey regained his balance and turned to charge again, coming between the bleak's raised sword and the foolish dog, who was still trying to advance on the creature, growling and curling back his lips.

"Fabio!" Daniella shrieked. "Leave it!"

Whether the hound was choosing to obey or simply reconsidered his position between the monstrous dragon and the ferocious bleak, Fabio fortunately tucked his tail down and retreated, fleeing to Daniella's side.

The bleak took this as a small victory and its eyes glowed beneath its dark brow as it danced forward with its sword upraised.

CHAPTER 21

Fabio's presence was surprisingly comforting… considering Daniella was watching a nightmarish creature from another world batter at her boyfriend the dragon. She clung to the dog and he whined so quietly that she could just feel it through his sides.

The curtain rod she'd dropped earlier had rolled over behind the counter and Daniella reached to pick it up.

It was noisy in the warehouse, all echoing roars and great wings flapping like sails and the bleak had a cackle of triumph that made the blood in Daniella's veins run cold.

"No!" she could not help crying, as Trey stumbled and the bleak darted forward to attack.

Strangely, the sound of her voice seemed to arrest the dark figure. Only for a moment, it seemed to wince and slow, as if her single shouted word had *hurt* it.

It was talking to the people in the diner…and the charging line order cook at the truck stop…that was what had stopped the dours. They'd shivered back away from her voice, and even the bleak was affected, though it was swinging its sword again, and Trey wasn't getting out of the way fast enough. They weren't just animals with a fear of human speech as Daniella had suspected, her speech was something that sapped their *power*.

And if she could hurt them by speaking, what could she do with singing? Daniella suddenly wondered, and she remembered Trey giving her the confidence to sing again, like a gift. She loved him, for all his strengths and weaknesses, for giving her the gift of song again.

She slowly stood, abandoning what little shelter the counter was giving her, opened her mouth and belted out the only song in her head, *I Saw Mommy Kissing Santa Claus*.

The song caught everyone by surprise, even Fabio, who craned his head around to look up at her curiously. But the bleak actually staggered in place and Trey rose up on his feet again as if he'd been re-energized. When the bleak pressed forward, its sword rebounded from Trey's scales without harming him. And this time, Trey's fire raked over him and ripped him into intangible shreds just as his claws did.

There was a curious sound in counterpart to her song, and it was a moment before Daniella recognized it as laughter—odd, draconian merriment, rumbling from Trey.

She smiled and planted her feet, lifting her chin to improve her breathing. The curtain rod might be laughable in her hand, but it was a solid weight. Then she launched into the second verse of the Christmas song, remembering with irony her edict to Trey that you couldn't sing Christmas songs after Christmas.

CHAPTER 22

Trey was not sure how much of his new energy was from the magic and light in Daniella's beautiful voice, and how much was relief and joy that he now had the power to protect her.

But while the bleak appeared to be incapable of damaging Trey any further, Trey seemed equally incapable of harming the bleak. They were both tiring, he thought, as they feinted and fought. Sword scraped against scale, and Trey dissolved the bleak repeatedly, but the only thing taking real damage was the building around them, already soundly trashed.

Then there was a great cracking sound and a portal ripped into existence in a far, dark corner of the warehouse. Trey and the bleak turned to it, both of them expecting a new enemy, and Daniella's golden song fell silent as she cleared her throat nervously.

The bleak's laugh of triumph was loud in the quiet room, and Fabio growled. "Now you lose, glass knight," it said confidently. "These are *my* people, and you and your key will fall and this rich, innocent world will become ours just as your world did."

Daniella drew a deep breath…and let it out in a squeak as a black mist of dours began to ooze into the warehouse through the portal, swirling across the floor towards the combatants. Behind the impossible mass of dours were taller figures—a gathered force of bleaks and worse, and they came menacingly towards the portal, unhurried and confident. This wasn't just a dispatch of fighters to deal with Trey and his key…this was an invasion force.

"Trey!" Daniella called hoarsely, just as there was a second cracking sound and another portal opened on the opposite side of the warehouse.

Trey swiveled, expecting to face more of the enemy at this closer portal.

A small, dark shape whizzed past him and Trey stopped himself from batting it out of the air at the last moment.

"Robin!" Daniella's voice was full of all the relief that Trey was feeling.

But Trey eyed the portal suspiciously—it was wastefully big for the diminished fable alone. A second figure tumbled out after Robin, a young woman bearing a sword and looking around with alarmed eyes. She took a step back as she looked up at Trey's dragon form, nearly falling back through the portal before Robin closed it.

"Got you that sword you wanted!" Robin said merrily. "And it looks like we're just in time."

The young woman saluted with her sword and settled into a practiced crouch, the blade before her. "Nice to meet you, I'm Gwen," she said with a faint southern accent, focusing her attention on the dours. "I understand you needed some assistance with pest control?"

The dours were still spilling out of the open portal

across the warehouse, swirling across the floor in a cold mist of darkness.

Trey drew in a breath and flamed into the dours, scattering them, but not harming them until Daniella added her voice to the cacophony in the echoing room, belting out another of her holiday tunes. Then, at last, the darkness started to shrivel away from his fire.

The swordbearer gave a high, loud "Kiyep!" and charged into the fray, slashing through the shadows.

"I can't hurt it!" Gwen cried as she fought, her sword sliding through the bleak like Trey's claws had. "Why can't I hurt it?"

"You haven't found your key yet," Robin called back to her. "You aren't at your full power yet, and it is."

"This bites!" Gwen observed angrily.

Despite her limitation, it was a rout in the best sense of the word; the dours melted before their assault, and the bleak army just beyond the portal hesitated… exactly long enough for Robin to send a sizzling spell that closed the rip between worlds on their angry and surprised faces.

The single remaining bleak in Daniella's world fought furiously, despite the change in energy. It backed into a corner with the last of the dours. Its sword was longer than Gwen's and the bleak was more skilled, but between Trey's song-strengthened flame and her ferocious attack, it was driven further and further back with each re-materialization.

"You won't save this world," it threatened in frustration. "Like your world, it will fall to us. You have won this year with surprise, but next year when the veil between these places grows thin again, we will return with a greater army, and we will put you in your place."

Then it reached behind itself with the sword and

pulled a portal out of nothing, abandoning the remaining dours to Trey's flame.

Trey expected it to simply flee, so he was surprised by the sound of crackling behind him, and Daniella's song ended in a gasp as she spun to meet the bleak stepping out of the portal behind her. Fabio surged up between them, barking furiously as the dark sword descended towards his head.

Trey launched himself into the air, trying to close the distance between them, but he knew he couldn't make it in time.

Daniella threw herself forward as Fabio yelped in pain and raised a brass rod that she was holding in her hands as she gave a wordless, musical cry. Trey roared. The rod pierced the bleak, who stared in surprise…as it stuck in his chest and simply stayed there.

The bleak didn't dissolve away uninjured, and it didn't re-materialize itself a few steps away.

It opened its mouth in protest and gave a burble of dismay, dropping its sword.

Daniella stood, still holding the other end of the rod and swaying in place, and the warehouse was eerily quiet. A piece of ceiling tile plummeted from above and raised a puff of dust among the swirling, confused dours who still remained, filling the shadows.

CHAPTER 23

After a moment of shock, Daniella finally let go of the curtain rod, which was solidly anchored in the shocked bleak's chest. They both dropped to their knees at the same time, on either side of Fabio, who was whining and snapping his jaws and shaking his head. Blood stained his pale fur.

The black sword fell from the bleak's hands and clattered to the floor as it toppled forward onto Fabio, who yelped in protest.

Daniella pushed at the limp bleak, trying to roll it off of a squirming Fabio. A rush of air preceded Trey's landing and Daniella looked up just in time to watch him shift back into human form and scramble from the counter to help her.

Together, they levered the bleak off of Fabio. There was a lot of blood, but he wiggled and tried to lick them as they inspected for damage.

"I think he's only lost an eartip," Trey declared at last. Fabio whined like he was in mortal pain and thumped his tail against the floor.

"You goon," Daniella said, her voice hoarse from unpracticed singing and nerves. She hugged Fabio tightly. "Is that thing... dead?"

Trey rolled it over and inspected it. The uncanny darkness that it had been composed of before seemed... weaker. More *melancholy gray* and less *blackness of lost souls*, Daniella thought. Fabio was licking her arm and trying to crawl into her lap. "You aren't a lap dog," she reminded him. "And you're bleeding on me." But she only cuddled him close, didn't try to push him away.

"It appears to be undone," Trey said in wonder as he touched the curtain rod. "Bleaks are powerful creatures," he said, touching the curtain rod curiously. "Your power is stronger than I realized."

"You were a pretty damned impressive dragon," Daniella pointed out.

Trey looked terribly pleased.

"Is the pupper okay?"

Daniella looked up to find a young Asian woman leaning over the counter. "He's going to be fine," she said in relief. "Just a flesh wound. I'm Daniella. This is Fabio."

"Gwen," the other woman introduced herself. "Tinkerbell here tells me I'm Henrik's key."

"Don't call me that!" Robin protested. "And I hate to break up the party, but there are still dours in the warehouse and if we don't mop them up before they get out, they *will* wreak havoc even if they aren't under the control of a bleak any longer. I'm also expecting that the witches on the other side may try another portal in while there are hours left in the day. I haven't got much power left, so if you could be of some *useful* assistance?"

Gwen vaulted over the counter and picked up the dark sword. "Will this do anything against the dours?"

"It's from their world, but there's only one way to find out," Trey told her.

Gwen grinned and swished the sword in the air. "Let's go see."

Daniella cautiously drew the curtain rod from bleak. It slid out easily and she paused, waiting to see if the bleak would reanimate, but instead it seemed to slump slowly into ash...though no ash actually remained behind.

For the next several hours, they chased slithering dours into dark corners and dispatched them. Fabio completely forgot his injured ear and dashed around the warehouse eagerly, barking and causing general chaos. The bleak's sword proved strong enough for Gwen to pin the dours, and either Tray could dissolve them with song-strengthened flame, or Daniella could skewer them with her blunt curtain rod.

There was a nerve-wracking moment when a sizzling sound like a portal broke the silence and the air began to split. Fabio howled and Robin sent a crackling counterspell to stop it in its tracks...then dropped from the air where they'd been hovering.

"Hope they don't try again," Robin whispered, when Daniella ran to gather them up from the concrete floor. "That's all I've got."

It seemed odd and presumptuous to cuddle them into her arms even though she was tempted. Daniella found a pile of random clothing and made Robin a comfortable nest on the counter.

"Could they portal somewhere else?" Daniella asked anxiously, thinking about the cafe, where the New Year's Eve party was probably in full swing.

"This is where we came through from our world," Robin said faintly. "It's going to be the easiest place for them."

"Like a sweater," Gwen suggested. "After you've put your finger through the weave."

Robin nodded wearily. They looked…smaller. Weaker.

Daniella looked at her watch. "And it all…resets? With the New Year?" It was only a few hours away, and it seemed like lifetimes.

"Last year, it was almost instantly impenetrable," Robin said reassuringly.

He fell into a fitful doze while the rest of them cornered all the remaining dours and searched around the building for traces of any that had slithered through the still-gaping hole in the wall. They could hear distant sounds of merriment through the cold night.

"Does your world have holidays every week?" Trey asked in bewilderment as they made a last circuit of the outside of the building.

"Not every week," Daniella said, shaking her head. "You just caught us at a busy holiday time. The next real holiday isn't until February."

"What does February celebrate?" Trey asked, poking her curtain rod into a shadowed hole half-covered with snow.

"February is the name of the month," Daniella explained. "The holiday is Valentine's Day."

"What is Valentine's?"

Daniella considered. "I think Valentine himself was a saint, but the day has very little to do with religion anymore. It's another one of those holidays that has evolved into giving each other gifts--usually chocolates and roses. It's about celebrating love, but where Christmas is about family love, Valentine's Day is about…romantic love."

Trey gave her a lopsided grin over his shoulder. "I like the sound of this holiday."

Daniella took his jacket lapels in her hands after he had convinced himself there was no dour lurking in the hole and stood up. "Trey..."

"My key?"

It was a curious endearment, but it warmed Daniella to her toes. "You have some explaining to do for me, for once," she observed. "But I wanted to say...I love you."

His face was so unexpectedly open, so expressive. His smile widened, the muscles of his cheeks changed, his eyes went soft and somehow deeper. "I love you, Daniella."

Then his mouth was over hers and Daniella knew she was home. Home in his arms, whatever world they ended up in.

CHAPTER 24

Only duty kept Trey from laying Daniella down in the slushy snow and making love her right then and there. Duty and the fact that it was a cold, wet bed. Also, there was still a threat of grave consequence if the horrors from his world managed to portal through again.

So Trey reluctantly released Daniella's lips after a long, passionate kiss and they made their way back into the warehouse.

They did another circuit of the inside of the warehouse, convinced at last that no doors remained behind, and waited in anxious tension for the snapping sound of a new portal.

They pulled a motley assortment of furniture and all the whole pillows and blankets they could find into a central area, not so coincidentally setting things up so that they could sit looking over each others shoulders. Daniella found sodas in a tiny version of her fridge and passed them out. Robin dozed limply on the couch, Gwen sat cross-legged on chair, and Trey settled into a loveseat with Daniella snuggled under his arm. Fabio lay across her legs.

"So Gwen, where are you from?" Daniella asked, as if they were simply at a social gathering.

"South Carolina," she said, running her finger along the edge of the black sword curiously. "First generation American, my folks were from Korea. You?"

"Born and grew up here," Daniella said easily. "Thought about going away for college but never did."

"For music?" Gwen guessed.

Trey felt Daniella stiffen beneath his arm. "I considered it. It's not really a practical pursuit."

"You've got a gorgeous set of pipes," Gwen encouraged, and Daniella gave a subtle squirm of embarrassed pleasure.

"Thanks. You're pretty handy with a sword."

"I'm a black belt in Tang Soo Do. Sword was always my favorite! I honestly never saw it being a *useful* skill, though."

"We are grateful for your assistance," Trey told her gravely. "How did Robin find you?"

Gwen chuckled. "In any other circumstances, I would say the story was too crazy to believe, but..." She gave a little wave at the wrecked warehouse. "Robin says he... er... they intercepted a bleak who was dowsing for me... they had to explain both of those terms to me. They said I was Henrik's *key*, that I was necessary for Henrik to tap this world's power and be released. It sounded weirder and weirder, and then they ripped a hole in the world and brought me here and... I dunno. It beat out my other New Year's Eve plans."

"Henrik..." Trey breathed, his chest tightening. "Where is he?"

Gwen gave a little apologetic shrug. "I have no idea. Robin said he was still lost." They all looked at Robin, who was boneless and small in their nest of tiny blankets.

"What *is* a key?" Daniella asked, looking up at Trey.

Trey pursed his lips thoughtfully. "As Robin explained it to me, you are my anchor here. I come from a very different place, and I cannot tap the energy of your world without your help. You are the person best suited to my needs. And the closer our…connection, the more power I can draw."

Daniella squeezed him tighter at the word *connection*. "And the singing? I mean, I have a decent voice, but I've never been able to make someone invincible with it before."

"I believe it is a manifestation of your ability to draw power for me," Trey decided. "Some witches from our world use ritual or physical items to focus their abilities. I suspect that your voice is how you visualize the access to the leylines below us."

"Am I going to have to sing, too?" Gwen asked in horror. "Because believe me, no one wants *that*."

"It varies by person," Robin assured her, rousing. "You may have a very different way of interpreting and controlling the leylines."

"Are you recovered?" Trey asked anxiously.

Robin grimaced as they sat up. "Not so recovered that I think I'd have a chance to close a portal," they said soberly. "But I'll probably be fine if that doesn't happen. What time is it?"

Daniella looked at the clock on her wrist. "About ten minutes until midnight."

There was a tense moment as they all tried very hard not to think about what could go wrong in ten minutes.

"We should toast it," Daniella said impulsively, squirming out from Trey's embrace. He and Fabio followed her as she walked swiftly to one of the toppled aisles and began scrambling over the discarded rubble.

"Ah, here, some of the plastic ones are still in one piece. Fabio, stay back!" Stepping carefully over broken glass, she picked out three tumblers and then climbed over another toppled aisle to find a plastic cup from a child's tea set.

They poured soda into these new vessels, Robin grumbling a little but looking appreciative of their cup.

"Do you have a key of your own, Robin?" Gwen asked, pouring it full from her can.

"I am a fable," Robin said. "I shouldn't need one." But they said it thoughtfully, as if they weren't sure.

"Here we go," Daniella said, holding up her watch. "The final fifteen…ten…nine…"

"Eight!" Gwen joined in. "Seven!"

Trey and Robin added, "Six! Five! Four! Three! Two! One!"

Fabio barked, they all gave a tired cheer and took sips of their drinks. Robin slugged their tea cup of bubbles and fell over backwards. "It's done," they said wearily. "They couldn't get through now if they tried."

Everyone toasted again with their drinks and slumped into their seats as relief set in. Fabio's tail wagged a few beats and fell still. Somewhere outside, there were sounds of distant explosions, but neither Daniella nor Gwen seemed the slightest bit alarmed. "Fireworks," Daniella explained cryptically.

Then she pointed up at the hole in the roof, just in time to see a shower of colored sparks overhead.

"What happens now?" Gwen asked into the quiet. "I don't think I'm getting a portal home tonight."

"Nope," Robin confirmed, still lying on their back.

"Now we find Henrik," Trey said firmly.

"*Right* now?" Daniella said skeptically.

"Maybe not *right* now," Trey conceded, kissing her forehead.

"I don't know how I'm going to explain this," Daniella said, looking around at the wrecked warehouse as if she were seeing it with fresh eyes. "Ansel is going to *kill* me."

"He will not," Trey said confidently. He had no intention of losing her *now*. "I would not allow him to."

Then he could not resist kissing her, until Robin made a gagging noise and Gwen found a pillow to throw at them, and then there was a sudden crash at the front door that made them all leap up, throw off their blankets, and reach for weapons as Fabio jumped to his feet and started barking.

"Uh… Hi, Ansel," Daniella said sheepishly.

CHAPTER 25

*D*aniella could only guess how Ansel felt.

From outside, the warehouse wasn't badly damaged. Trey had come in through the roof, and though it was a gaping hole from inside and it was letting a view of the stars and a lot of cold, it wasn't visible from outside. The gap that had been knocked through the wall was on the backside of the building.

So it must have been a shock coming in.

None of the tall shelf aisles were still standing, and the whole building was strewn with merchandise. Most everything glass had been shattered. The sales counter was one of the few undamaged things. The jagged holes in the back wall and ceiling were letting all the cold night air in. Most of the lights had been broken, and the ones that still worked were flickering like a terrible low grade movie.

And in the center of the chaos, three people were standing in a loose half-circle: an Asian girl holding a dark sword upraised, a giant, well-built man with his fists balled up, and Daniella herself holding a tarnished brass curtain-rod. To say nothing of Robin, who had lifted themself into the air by sheer force of will, and Fabio, who had decided Ansel was a new friend and was bolting forward with his tongue flailing and his tail wagging.

"Guh!" Ansel said, pushing Fabio down. "What the hell is going on? What did you do to my *store*?" Then he spotted Robin and he scowled. "You! I've seen you here before, lurking around the merchandise. Are you some kind of *fairy*??"

Robin, realizing that it wasn't some new threat, dropped back out of the air onto the cushion. "Fable," they muttered sullenly, then fell over on their side in exhaustion.

"A couple of people told me they heard a commotion from the store. I figured I'd catch some kids sneaking off to drink and party…but this?"

Daniella swept her gaze around the warehouse. Nothing but the truth was going to explain the destruction. And the truth was utterly *crazy*.

"Come have a seat," she invited, putting her curtain rod down. "We'll explain everything."

"Do we want to do that?" Gwen asked skeptically. She lowered her sword and went to check on Robin, tucking a doll blanket around them carefully. Robin pushed her hand away crossly and sat up again, but they swayed wearily in place.

Daniella pulled Trey down to sit beside her on the couch, scooting over so that there was room for Ansel to sit because he didn't particularly look like he could remain standing much longer.

"This is Trey," she introduced. "He's from another world."

"Ah…" Ansel said. He seemed incapable of a spoken reply, but habit made him thrust out a hand for Trey to shake as he took a seat. Fabio tried to climb into his lap and satisfied himself with leaning against the man's legs adoringly when he was refused the space. He seemed to have forgotten his injured ear, and all of the blood in his blond fur was dried.

Trey had met enough people by now to shake the offered hand and say, "A pleasure to meet you."

"Robin is the fable, a creature made of magic," Daniella continued. "They are pretty worn out by helping us stop what caused all of this."

Trey looked sheepish as he let go of Ansel's hand. "I am afraid that I am to blame for most of the damage."

Ansel stared at him, then looked up, clearly measuring him against the hole in the roof and wall. Trey was a big man, but the ruin of the warehouse looked like nothing short of construction equipment could cause it.

"I'm a dragon," Trey explained matter-of-factly.

Ansel rubbed his hand through his short, blond hair. "I only had one drink," he said helplessly. "Just for the toast."

"Let's start at the beginning," Daniella said. "There's another world. Trey and Robin are from that world. There are bad things there, and they escaped here last year through a portal between these worlds. The bad things want to come here and take over our world like they did their world, and there's a weak place here where they first came through and it's the weakest of all right before New Year's. We stopped them, this time, but they'll try again next year, and we're going to need more help. With me so far?"

"I'm missing the part where he's a dragon," Ansel said, still sounding shocky. "Where's that part?"

"He's a dragon...er...shapeshifter. But his flame doesn't make fire, it makes...uh, Trey?"

"Light. Against the darkness. That is what we are," Trey explained. "My shieldmates and I were the last of our kind: half magic, half man. We stood against the darkness in the world as long as we could, but we were sadly outnumbered and out powered. Robin brought us here hoping only for refuge. But I fear we have endangered your world with our coming."

Ansel looked at Gwen. "What are you?"

"I'm just a person," Gwen said, spreading her hands helplessly. "I'm all new to this, too. Name's Gwen."

"Ansel," he told her numbly.

"Robin showed up at my place earlier today with crazy stories that I honestly didn't entirely believe until they ripped a hole in space and brought me here to fight a bunch of shadows with a dragon."

"In my warehouse."

"Yeah, sorry," Gwen said sheepishly. "I'm supposed to be the key for this guy's shieldmate, Henrik."

"Another dragon?"

"A gryphon."

"Sure." Ansel was taking everything in stride really well, Daniella thought. "What's a *key*?"

Daniella could answer that. "Sort of like a counterpart in this world. I'm Trey's key. His magic is weak here in this world, but I can give him…er…power. When I sing, particularly." It still sounded insane. "He has three other shieldmates. They were caught in a trap that turned them all to glass before Robin could save them and bring them here."

"Four of them?" Ansel asked sharply. "Turned to glass? Like glass ornaments?"

Everyone stared at him and sat up straighter.

"Last year," he said, shaking his head. "Last year, I found four glass ornaments on the floor when I came in after New Year's. No idea where they came from, no one ever claimed them."

Robin stood up, and nearly fell over. "Where are they now?" they asked plaintively.

Trey leaned towards Ansel urgently. "My shieldmates? Here?" His glance raked the warehouse and Daniella knew he was wondering if they had been unknowingly shattered in the battle.

"I...uh...sold them," Ansel said apologetically. "Honestly, it was a miracle they weren't broken, but otherwise, they didn't seem magical. Just...pretty glass ornaments."

Trey took him by the shoulders. "Who did you sell them to?" he demanded. "Where are they?!"

"They were...gosh, it was almost a year ago," Ansel said, shrinking back in alarm as Trey loomed over him. "Nobody local; we get a lot of antique deal hunters through town."

Daniella pulled Trey back by the arm. "They'd be in the ledger, right?"

"The sale, sure," Ansel said. "But I don't have a lot of information about customers. I'll look, see if it jogs anything, but it's not like I have a photographic memory, and not everyone just volunteers where they're from."

"It's a place to start," Daniella said peacefully.

CHAPTER 26

Trey felt hope choke him. His shieldmates *had* made it safely into this world. He was not alone. He felt Daniella's arms tighten around him and knew that even if he never found them, he had found the one person who completed him.

He turned and gave her a quick, desperate embrace. "We must find them," he said firmly. "We must find them before next year when the world veil grows thin."

"That's a lot of time," Daniella told him, and her arms were a comfort. "We can use the Internet, and once Robin is rested, they can try dowsing for Henrik and the other shieldmates again. You said that Trey's dragon might help with that, didn't you, Robin?"

"Might help," Robin said with a yawn. "Dowsing's kind of sloppy at the best of times. It won't be soon."

Gwen looked between them. "So...what *now?*"

Daniella caught Robin's yawn and her jaw cracked. "You can come stay at my house," she offered, once she'd escaped the reflex. "It's a small place, but you can sleep on the couch."

"I've got a spare room," Ansel offered unexpectedly, his voice gruff. "You'll have to move some boxes, but it sounds like you might be around a few days."

"You're pretty generous for someone who just got his business trashed," Gwen observed skeptically.

"You're pretty calm for someone who just got yanked through a hole from South Carolina to save the world," Ansel countered.

"Touché," Gwen chuckled. "I accept."

"What are we going to do about this place?" Daniella asked quietly.

"I am happy to help repair whatever I can," Trey offered at once, knowing too well his part in the destruction.

"Like you said, I'll be around for a few days at least," Gwen said wryly. "Might as well help out."

"Am I going to be fired?" Daniella asked with a giggle.

Ansel looked thoughtful, stroking a grateful Fabio's head. "That many hands, clean-up shouldn't be too bad. I'll get some supplies at the hardware store tomorrow, but a lot of these shelves just look they were knocked over. Ought to be able to right them and salvage a lot of the merchandise. Glassware's a dead loss, but the clothes should be fine once they're laundered. Some furniture is gone, I'll have to hire someone to repair the roof. Think I can claim a meteor, once I clean up the rest of it?"

"It might not pass an insurance inspection, but James Tilly won't ask questions if you hire him in cash," Daniella suggested.

"And hey, it's a hell of a tax write-off, because it happened before the end of the fiscal year!" Ansel added. "You'll have to do the inventory over, though..."

Daniella yawned again. "How about tomorrow?"

"It'll keep," Ansel agreed.

"Shall we retire until then?" Trey suggested.

They all stood. Gwen kept the blanket wrapped around her, shivering.

Trey clapped Ansel on the shoulder, perhaps a little too hard. "We shall adjourn in the morn," he said cheerfully. They had a mission, a purpose. He would repair the warehouse, and then he and Daniella and the warrior Gwen would begin the search for his shieldmates.

He went to lift Robin. "You're not carrying me like a baby, lizard-breath," they told him, with a reassuring amount of their usual vigor. "I'll sit on your shoulder."

Fabio pranced around underfoot, whining in excitement. He, of all of them, seemed least bothered by the great battle they had just fought. His ear didn't seem to hurt at all.

"I live just down the street," Ansel was explaining to Gwen. "It's a short walk, but it's cold out. You want a coat or…er…some pants?"

"It was sixty degrees at home," she lamented. "Pants would be lovely." They went to investigate the toppled clothing aisles.

"See you tomorrow," Daniella called.

Then he and Daniella went out into the bracing cold. Trey wished he'd been wearing a coat when he shifted, but he wasn't going to admit that to Daniella. Robin was an insulated spot on his shoulder, still wrapped in the doll blanket that Gwen had found for them.

They walked briskly, Fabio capering before them.

"Happy New Year's," Daniella said, holding tight to his unencumbered arm. "I'm glad we'll have a little…respite."

"Daniella," Trey said slowly.

"I really hope we can find your shieldmates," she said too hastily, not looking up at him.

Trey drew her to a stop. "Daniella," he repeated, ignoring his chill.

She finally looked at him, and she could see all the worry and weariness that was crashing down inside her. Fabio, sensing his mistress' distress, returned to press between them.

"I know you want to go back. To save your world. I'd… come with you. We could do that, right?"

Trey put a finger over her mouth. "Daniella," he said a final time. "My world is gone, the people there that I knew no longer exist. Even with my shieldmates at my side, I am not foolish enough to fight a battle that is already lost. *This* is my world now, and my place is by your side, guarding it."

"I heard you tell Robin…"

"Who is right here," the fable reminded them from Trey's shoulder, sounding crabby. "So no squishy stuff."

"I wanted to go back," Trey said frankly. "Before I understood the scope of what had happened, and the danger to this world. I caused this danger, in part, and it is my duty to protect it…but it is my joy to stay at your side. I…would not return even if I could, my key."

"Your shieldmates…" Daniella said faintly.

"They may wish to return if we find them," Trey said, nodding. "But if they do, it will be without me. I belong here."

And then, even Robin's protests couldn't keep him from stooping to kiss Daniella, and she kissed him back.

"You're cold," she chided, stepping back with tears in her eyes. "And I think Robin is going to bite you. Let's go home."

Fabio heard the word home and led the way, his glorious fur rippling against the wind as he ran before them.

EPILOGUE

*R*obin had a headache.
Headache was a slight misnomer, since as a fable, they had none of the usual nerve endings or veins or muscles that would cause a human headache. They were made of magic, and lacked…Robin laughed slightly, wincing. Lacked *everything* human.

They had no gender, no human mass constraints, no sense of pain or injury.

But being drained of magic left a hollow, horrid feeling that had Robin reeling. It wasn't mere weakness, it was something deeper, something where their bones might be. They thought it must be like pain, and it seemed to center where they were trying to think, so they called it a headache.

"Do you need anything?"

Robin opened their eyes. After more than a year now, it was always still a surprise when someone leaned over them, giant-huge, in a world that was all the wrong sizes. Daniella's gentle face was sweet, and her brown eyes worried. Robin suspected that people didn't realize how expressive they were, when every little twist and twitch was telegraphed at this size.

"No, but I thank you," they said, and the magic deficit was such that even the effort of speech felt Herculean. They were grateful that the effect ran both ways; Daniella would not pick up on their own expressions, shrunk as they were to such a size.

Daniella fussed over them anyway, picking up the doll blanket that had fallen to the floor. Robin was set up on the counter in a chair for a doll that might have been a good size before their battle. Now, drained further than they'd ever dared, they had diminished again overnight, and where they had been small, now they were *tiny*.

"It would have been quieter to stay home with Fabio," Daniella scolded them gently, the concern in her eyebrows like giant bears.

Robin had considered that, but with no strength left to portal, they'd wanted to stay close to Trey, the last of their shieldmates. "I am fine," they said, more strongly, trying to project confidence they didn't feel. "Only tired. I want to be here in case we find any clues that only I could sense." They doubted their ability to be of actual use, in their current state, but Trey's magic had always been rather ham-handed and insensitive, and perhaps they could at least advise.

Daniella returned to her work.

Trey and the humans were picking through the aftermath of the battle, righting shelves and sweeping up piles of glass and rubble. Cold winter sunlight spilled in through the rent roof, and they all wore gloves and scarves and hats. Robin was dressed in ill-fitting doll clothing, wrapped in layers of home-knit blankets. They didn't feel cold any more than they felt pain, but being wrapped in things seemed to make the *others* feel better, and there was something comforting in having weight about them.

It was a reminder that they hadn't diminished to *nothing* yet, at least. Robin was beginning to consider that was an unpleasant possibility.

"This is toast," Gwen said, lifting something familiar out of the trash.

It was a dollhouse, crushed and folded, and Robin felt a wave of grief.

They had spent many nights in that place, taking comfort in something their own size, sitting at the tables and chairs, pretending that they weren't slowly starving in this world of strange, reluctant magic as they worked to free Trey.

Gwen carried the broken plastic house to the growing trash pile and Robin winced as it crashed into the heap. It was joined by a bent baby swing, and shards of plastic toys. She fluffed a stuffed animal, brushing debris from its fur, and added it to the pile of things to be washed.

The front door crashed open. "I've got take-out!" Ansel yelled, coming in with several plastic bags straining around carry-out containers.

"I think I love you!" Gwen called out merrily, coming to clear off a portion of counter near Robin to lay out the food.

Trey and Daniella left what they were working on and came to open containers and sniff curiously.

"What manner of food is this?" Trey asked raptly, letting Daniella pile things onto his paper plate.

"This is Chinese food," Daniella explained. "Well, it's probably very American Chinese food. But it's good." She made Robin a small serving on one of the soup lids, and Robin gratefully sucked down noodles nearly the length of their body and a partial nugget of breaded sweet and sour chicken. They were able to eat in this world, as they had in their own, but the energy they got from it was more complicated and less effective than pure magic.

While they ate, Daniella and Gwen explained geography to Trey. They found most of a globe in the trash pile and pointed out major features. They searched for the little town they were in, and the city that Gwen had come from. Ansel pointed out where he'd gone to school, and Gwen found the city her parents had immigrated from.

"It's not quite like our world," Trey observed, setting aside his empty plate. "Some of the shapes are almost familiar, but... not quite. If this were our kingdom, here, there would be another large continent, here."

"Atlantis," Gwen suggested, but her voice was teasing. She was eating gracefully with chopsticks, her feet propped up on a chair in front of her. Ansel was sitting in a recliner with a definite cast to one side next to her. Daniella and Trey were sitting as close to each other as they could on the little loveseat, occasionally feeding each other tidbits from their plates.

Trey missed the Atlantis reference, but Daniella giggled. Robin had been able to absorb enough of the culture to know what she was talking about.

While they explained Atlantis and its mythology to Trey, Robin finished their food. It wasn't as nourishing as magic, and did nothing for their size, but they felt a little better. Less hungover.

"We should get back to it," Daniella said reluctantly, looking around at the mess that still needed dealt with.

"Having a dragon has been useful," Ansel said. "You've gotten further than I thought you would."

"Too bad we can't let the dragon haul these things to the dump," Gwen said, eyeing the large trash heap.

"Maybe after dark?" Trey suggested hopefully.

"Best not," Robin said. "Not with everyone around here carrying visual recorders in their pockets." He set aside the empty soup lid.

"Can you imagine how viral that would go?" Gwen said.

"Maybe it would get the right person's attention?" Daniella suggested. "If another of your shieldmates has been released?"

"Not worth the risk," Robin said firmly. "If someone took it upon themselves to put Trey in a cage, we'd be desperately short-handed next year."

Trey made a proud, skeptical noise.

"You haven't seen enough movies yet," Robin told him. "Throw enough government agencies at you, and you'll be in a basement in no time, pumped full of experimental drugs and chained to the floor."

Ansel gave him a narrow-eyed look. "You know, I could not figure out why my Netflix stats kept getting mixed up. I changed my password every few weeks."

Robin gave him a grin. "But you'd log in with the new password at the store every time, so it didn't do much good."

Ansel shook his head, chuckling. "You had me questioning my sanity a lot this past year," he said, exasperated. "I bet you're the cause of a lot of my weird browser history, too."

"You know, viral isn't the worst thought, actually. What if we made a Craigslist post?" Daniella mused. "We can describe the other ornaments, post a photo of Trey's, write a heart-wrenching story about how we're looking for heirlooms in this matched set and will pay any price."

"My darling deceased grandma Nettie's glass gryphon!" Gwen teased, twirling her chopsticks, but Robin, hypersensitive to everyone's expressions, thought she seemed a little concerned. She had only had a day to get used to the idea of being Henrik's key and she seemed to be taking everything as well as could be expected, but Robin knew that this whole circus was a lot to take in, and they could see the stress in her neck and the drape of her foot.

Ansel shrugged. "The idea has merit. We can narrow down when they were each sold, maybe get it shared on Facebook?"

"It's a start," Robin agreed.

With unspoken consensus, they all finished their food and rose to throw away their plates and start in again on cleaning up the mess from the night before.

Robin watched them helplessly, pulling the blankets closer around them for the comfort of it.

They all worked cheerfully, blissfully unaware of their easy strength and grace, sorting piles of trash, sweeping piles of glass, cautioning each other when they found hazards in the heaps.

Daniella and Trey worked as close together as they could manage, glancing at each other often, and frequently exchanging touches; brushing hips, or just casually reaching out as if neither one of them could resist. She sang at times, to the radio, or to the music in her own head, and the power between the two was palpable when she did. It wasn't just attraction; they gravitated to each other like stars, and their joy and contentment in the connection was so obvious that even the other humans felt it.

Gwen watched the two of them, her face furrowed in concentration and that underlying concern. Robin suspected she was wondering what it would mean to find Henrik, whether she would have that same jubilant partnership with him. There was longing there, and doubt.

Ansel worked in a daze, clearly questioning the life decisions that had lead to the destruction of his shop and frequently shaking his head in disbelief.

Robin pitied him; they'd grown to like Ansel over the time they'd used the second hand store as a home base, and they felt bad for the trouble he'd been unwittingly dragged into. Daniella and Gwen had been destined for this fight. Ansel had just owned real estate in the wrong place.

Robin frowned, facing the possibility that they would never find Henrik. Who knew how far he'd traveled by now, whether his glass prison was even still whole. When Robin had dowsed for the gryphon knight, all they had found was Gwen.

Trey and the humans worked until the hole in the roof began to darken with the sky, and the cold became sharper.

"Let's go to Marie's," Daniella suggested, as they regathered at the counter near Robin, stomping their feet and blowing on their hands. "My treat."

Robin stood. They felt marginally better, though they didn't have to try any magic to know that they would be incapable of it.

There was a murmur of agreement, then Daniella looked awkwardly at Robin. "We can't exactly bring…"

"I have spent many meals eating candy bar crumbles in the corners of forgotten shelves or trapped in trees trying to escape dogs," Robin said serenely. "I assure you it will be a great improvement if you can leave me at your house with a television remote in reach."

"Of course," Daniella said promptly. "We'll make you a snack, and I'd like to shower before going out anyway."

"You can shower at my place," Ansel said to Gwen, with a casual shrug of one shoulder.

Gwen's reply was just as offhand. "Sure! Let me write you an IOU for a change of clothing." She had collected a few items of clothing that would fit her as they sorted the rubble, and Robin was reminded again that they had snatched her from her home without a change of clothing or a wallet, and were incapable of returning her to her life in the near future.

They stared unhappily at their palms until Trey offered his big hands to lift them to the dragon knight's shoulder. While he waited for Daniella to finish with something, he asked in a quiet rumble, "Robin, are you better?"

"Better," Robin said, sitting with all the dignity they could muster on Trey's broad shoulder. "The magic here... it's like sucking a milkshake that is too thick through a tiny straw."

Trey gave a chuckle. "I get that reference!" he said warmly. "I've had a milkshake! It gave me...*brain*freezing!"

They walked home in the deepening darkness, Robin gazing around at the peaceful world they'd ended up in. Their worries here were trivial—no one fretted over the inevitable loss of their loved ones to endless darkness, no one wondered when the armies of dours would appear to pit them against each other. It was still and beautiful and...hopeful.

Robin couldn't remember a time when they'd felt hope like everyone here took for granted.

They vowed to protect it to the best of their ability... then remembered despondently that they were capable of *nothing* now.

There was a box waiting on Daniella's front steps, and she let go of Trey's hand to inspect it. "Oh, Robin! This is for you!" she said in delight.

Robin nearly fell from Trey's shoulder. "For me?"

Trey was grinning broadly.

"It's late for Christmas," Daniella said apologetically, "but Trey wanted to do something for you, and I did, too."

There was a moment of happy chaos as Trey and Daniella tried to get into the house with the box, and Fabio tried to get out of the house and lick everyone, all at the same time.

Then Robin was being put on the kitchen table and Daniella was cutting open the box with a knife and lifting out the contents as Trey and Fabio watched eagerly.

"Sorry it isn't wrapped," Daniella said merrily.

"Next year, we will wrap gifts," Trey said firmly. "You will have to show me how."

Within the box were many smaller boxes, and they all opened to reveal things just Robin's size. Or, at least, their size of the night before.

"They're still at least a better fit than my furniture," Daniella said, pulling the bubblewrap off of a small desk chair. "We'll set you up with your own place out of Fabio's reach and build you some walls for privacy. We can give it a rope ladder for when you aren't up for flying."

There was a sturdy desk, with a drawer that actually pulled out, the matching desk chair, a padded love seat (that could currently serve as a bed, given Robin's size), a battery-powered lamp with a tiny real bulb in it, a bed with a Christmas quilt, a small dresser, and a selection of clothing - skirts and pants and shirts and coats and tiny socks. There was even a small plush bear, about the size of Robin's torso.

It was all slightly the wrong scale, but not nearly as wrong a scale as everything else, and it took Robin a moment to identify the feelings welling in their chest. They were grateful, and they were grief-stricken, and they were glad.

"You do me great honor," they said gravely. "I am indebted to you."

"You did just save the world," Daniella reminded them.

"You did much of that yourself," Robin protested, holding up an outfit. The skirts, in particular, would keep them decent and flex with their size well as they slowly regained their strength...or what they could of it in this world.

"Oh!" Daniella remembered. "One more thing." She vanished into her bedroom and reemerged with a phone in her hand. "This is my old phone. It's not fancy, and it's slow, and it doesn't have a sim card, but it will work with my wifi, and you can use it as a computer. It's fine to browse the Internet, listen to music. Oh, er, don't judge me by my playlists. I didn't wipe it yet."

"I would not dream of passing judgment," Robin said truthfully.

The phone was nearly as big as they were, but Daniella found a way to prop it up so that they could use it and gave them the unlock code. "We'll hook up the charger permanently when we get you set up with the rest of your house."

A house of their own. Privacy. Respect.

Robin thanked them profusely, not even sure of the words they were saying around the choking emotions in their diminished body.

Pleased by their response, Trey tipped his giant forehead gently against Robin's, and Daniella dropped a fond kiss on the top of their head. Then they scurried off to take a swift shower and Robin was alone with their own confused thoughts.

They sat thoughtfully in the chair, their legs dangling. The chair even swiveled, though it was a little stiff and he had to push off from the table to turn.

As a fable, made of magic, Robin lacked everything human. They had no organs or blood, they felt no human pain, experienced no human weaknesses, even if their magical deficit mimicked some of those symptoms.

But within their chest, within their very soul, was a very human heart.

And right now, that heart was the largest part of them, filled with an unexpected love. They had always been fond of their shieldmates, but it had been duty that had driven them. They had trained the four knights out of obligation, out of… programming.

Now, there was more than duty.

Now, for the first time in much longer than Robin liked to admit, there was *hope*. This was a world worth protecting, full of selfless people who deserved better than the darkness they feared was coming.

Whatever it took, however they diminished, they had a cause now, and a battle they were willing to sacrifice everything to win.

~

Robin felt better the following morning, though they weren't appreciably larger. The nagging hollow-bones feeling was less, and the exhaustion seemed more distant. They didn't sleep, exactly, but they did drowse to restore energy, and it was pleasant to have a bed of their own, at least close to their scale. It was better than nesting in a forgotten corner of the second hand store hoping that no one needed socks from the bottom of the basket.

They lay in their bed for some time after they heard Daniella get up and let Fabio out, and tested their wells of magic.

They got up with a sigh. It would be days, maybe weeks, before they could manage a portal, or do dowsing at any distance, but it was flying that they missed most.

They ate breakfast with Daniella and Trey, Fabio begging at the foot of the table. It was lovely to have a table of their own to sit at, rather than holding their food awkwardly in their lap.

It had snowed overnight, and when they arrived at the second hand store, Gwen was sweeping out a drift of snow that had come in through the hole in the roof.

"Good morning," she called cheerfully. "You look better, Tinkerbell."

That was for Robin, who thought that flipping her off was an appropriate response.

Ansel was making phone calls, pacing around as he talked, and everyone else dug back into the clean-up work.

Robin paced the counter and used Ansel's computer to search nearby news for any indication that their battle had spilled out of the warehouse, looking for reports of violence and unrest. They were relieved to find nothing more than casual reports of post-New Year's drinking detentions and lost dogs. There had been a small fire set by careless fireworks, but the fire department had swiftly put it out.

"I'm not going to be able to get the roof repaired for about a week," Ansel said regretfully, when everyone had assembled for a break. "We should get a tarp over that hole, in the meantime."

They all frowned thoughtfully upwards. "I'm not really very good with heights," Gwen confessed. "I'd be a liability up there."

"I am excellent with heights," Trey said modestly.

They were probably all thinking how useful it would be

to have him able to help in dragon form, but no one suggested it.

A tall ladder and a tarp were unearthed from one of the heaps of rubble, and Ansel, Daniella, and Trey went to the top of the warehouse to anchor and support it with scrap lumber from behind the building.

It was curious, listening to them bang around overhead. The acoustics of the warehouse were wretched, at best, and every footstep and rustle, and the occasional shouted direction, echoed through the room.

Robin gave Gwen an appraising look as she brought a heavy bucket of broken glass and bits of toys and dishes to dump into the very full trash can. "Have you been able to get in touch with your family?" they asked.

"I called my brother last night on Ansel's phone," Gwen said, letting the shards flow slowly into the gaps of the trash with a musical clatter against the metal can. She came to perch on a stool that had been repaired with duct tape. "He's going to express mail my wallet and phone. He's pretty sure I've lost my mind, but he's a good brother who knows I can kick his ass, so he'll smooth things over with my folks. I talked to my roommate so she can start looking for a new renter for next month, and I quit my job. If you're not up for portaling before the end of the month, I can use my airline miles, but I was hoping to save them for a flight in case Henrik showed up in Mexico or something."

Robin frowned at her, sitting on an upside down cup. It wasn't that they were tired, exactly, just that standing up seemed like more effort than they wanted to be expending. "You're just… leaving your life?"

Gwen leaned over the counter, her dark eyes deep and thoughtful as she cupped her chin in her hands. "I've spent that whole life feeling like I was waiting for something, that there was more than slinging coffee and teaching kids the first forms. When you showed up, something... clicked. I mean, I'm not going to say that I wasn't pretty doubtful until you ripped a door in space time to a *dragon* battle, or that there aren't still moments when I wonder if this isn't all some crazy hallucination. But...this feels right. It's where I belong. I can do some *good* here."

"You are Henrik's key," Robin said approvingly. "I look forward to training you."

She gazed down, then asked shyly, "What's he like?"

"He is a gryphon," Robin said thoughtfully. "He is a warrior of light. He is a good man. He is an excellent fighter."

Gwen's expression telegraphed her dissatisfaction with their description, but Robin knew they couldn't tell her what she really wanted to know: would she love him the way that Daniella loved Trey? Uncertainty was brilliant over her features.

"If my so-called magic isn't activated by song like Daniella's is, how *does* it work?" Gwen asked.

Robin gave a helpless shrug. "We'll have to figure it out as we go. I can train you in our magic and fighting methods and see if something clicks for you. We have a whole year to figure it out, and a lot can happen in a year."

"And it's possible that I won't be able to figure anything out until we find Henrik," Gwen suggested.

"That's also possible."

Gwen straightened, brushing off her hands. "Then I guess we've got a gryphon to find." She paused, and then dipped her head towards Robin. Robin leaned forward and touched their small forehead to hers, feeling a wave of hope. Then she was whistling, off-tune, back to her work.

Robin smiled slowly. They had a year to train her in magic, to find Henrik and with luck, even the other shieldmates. Maybe Robin could find a way to permanently seal the veil between their worlds. Maybe they could find a way to tap the magic of this world more cleanly. Maybe they could find or create their own key.

A lot could happen in a year.

And they would be ready.

∼

*C*ontinue the story in Unicorn of Glass or read on for a sneak preview! I also have a free story, Burn Offerings, available on my webpage - shortly after Dragon of Glass, Trey attempts to cook for Daniella. ...It goes badly. (Join my mailing list for more bonus stories and extras!)

A NOTE FROM ZOE

Thank you for reading my book! I hope you enjoyed Daniella and Trey's adventures.

This cover was done by Ellen Million. Visit her site for sketches of my characters and signed bookplates! The ornament on the cover was commissioned specifically for this book from A Touch of Glass. Their webpage is: glass4gifts.com

I always love to know what you thought – you can leave a review at Amazon or Goodreads or email me at zoechantebooks@gmail.com.

If you'd like to be emailed when I release my next book, please click here to be added to my mailing list. You can also visit my webpage, where I have a complete book list by series, or follow me on Facebook or Twitter.

Readers like you are why I write, and I am so grateful for all of your support.

~Zoe

MORE BY ELVA BIRCH

A Day Care for Shifters: A hot new full-length series about adorable shifter kids and their struggling single parents in a town full of mystery and surprise. Start the series with Wolf's Instinct, when Addison comes to Nickel City to take a job at a very special day care and finds a family to belong to. A gentle ice-cream-straight-from-the-container escape. Sweet and sizzling!

The Royal Dragons of Alaska: A fascinating alternate world where Alaska is ruled by secret dragon shifters. Adventure, romance, and humor! Reluctant royalty, relentless enemies…dogs, camping, and magic! Start with The Dragon Prince of Alaska.

∾

Suddenly Shifters: A hilarious series of novellas, serials, and shorts set in the small town of Anders Canyon, where something (in the water?) is making ordinary citizens turn into shifters. Start with Something in the Water!

∾

Lawn Ornament Shifters: The series that was only supposed to be a joke, this is a collection of short, ridiculous romances featuring unusual shifters, myths, and magic. Cross-your-legs funny and full of heart! Start with The Flamingo's Fated Mate!

∾

Birch Hearts: An enchanting collection of short stories and novellas. Unconstrained by theme or setting, each short read has romance, magic, and heart, with a satisfying conclusion. And always, the impossible and irresistible. Start with a sampler plate in Prompted 2 for fourteen pieces of sweet-to-sizzling flash fiction, or dive in with the novella, Better Half - which you can get free for joining my mailing list at elvabirch.com!

MORE BY ZOE CHANT

Shifting Sands Resort: A complete ten-book series - plus two collections of shorts. This is a thrilling shifter romance set at a tropical island resort. Each book stands alone but connects into a great mystery with a thrilling conclusion. Start with Tropical Tiger Spy or dive in to the Omnibus edition, with all of the novels, short stories, and novellas in my preferred reading order!

∽

Fae Shifter Knights: A complete four-book fantasy portal romp, with cute pets and swoon-worthy knights stuck in a world of wonders like refrigerators and ham sandwiches. Start with Dragon of Glass!

∽

Green Valley Shifters: A sweet, small town series with single dads, secret shifters, sweet kids, and spinsters. Lowperil and steamy! Standalone books where you can revisit your favorite characters - this series is also complete with six books! Start with Dancing Bearfoot! This series crosses over with **Virtue Shifters**, which starts with Timber Wolf.

BEHIND THE SCENES

What is Patreon?

Patreon is a site where readers and fans can support creators with monthly subscriptions.

At my Patreon, I have tiers with early rough drafts of my books, flash fiction, coloring pages, signed and sketched paperbacks, exclusive swag, original artwork, photographs…and so much more! Every month is a little different, and there is a price for every budget. Patreon allows me to do projects that aren't very commercial and makes my income stream a little less unpredictable. It also gives me a place to connect with my fans!

Come find out what's going on behind the scenes and keep me creating at Patreon! patreon.com/ellenmillion

UNICORN OF GLASS, CHAPTER 1

The Christmas bell by the door jingled as Heather came in, Vesta prancing happily at her feet. The holiday chime might be an odd sound to hear in July, but not nearly as odd as the Christmas music inside. Heather was sweating in the humid Georgia heat, even though they had only ducked out into it for a moment. Matters were not at all helped by the heavy green velvet 'elf' dress she was wearing. She peeled the fake fur back from her neck as she stepped into the frigid air conditioning.

It was probably ninety outside and comparatively it felt like fifty inside, though the thermostat behind the counter showed a perfectly livable seventy.

"I'm back!" Heather hollered towards the back of the store, pouring water from her bottle into the dog bowl underneath the register. Vesta lapped it up eagerly and crawled onto the pillow next to it, her wiry little tail beating out a rhythm as she settled down to nap at Heather's feet.

"We got a box!" Julie crowed, coming from the back

room of the shop just as Heather observed the delivery waiting on the counter. "Who gets to open it?"

Fred and Angie, the owners of the Ornament Shoppe, spent most of the summer touring the country in an RV, finding kitschy Christmas-themed treasure from all over the world in antique shops and at flea markets. Most of it came home with them in the fall in a trailer, but through the summer, they would ship some of it back.

Some of the things that Fred and Angie found defied belief: a horrifying wind-up laughing Santa Claus whose head popped off in a spray of red ribbons, a team of reindeer made entirely made of spoons and forks, a nativity scene made of metal dinosaurs, a can of Christmas turkey from the forties...and there were always new ornaments.

The Ornament Shoppe claimed it carried more ornaments than any other shop in the world, though Heather privately wondered if that was a statement that ever could or would be proven. It certainly had a *lot*. There were wooden ornaments, blown glass ornaments, metal ornaments, cheap plastic ornaments, popsicle-stick ornaments, cloth ornaments, papercraft ornaments, and balls of plastic and glass.

There was an entire aisle of Hallmark collectibles, and rows of weird geeky ornaments for television shows that had been off the air for decades, ethnic ornaments from all over the world, handmade ornaments, one-of-a-kind ornaments, even mechanical ornaments.

If there was an animal, no matter how obscure or imaginary, they had an ornament for it. If there was a hobby or sport, they had an ornament for it. They even had a Santaur ornament, with a half-horse, half-naked, disturbingly sexy Santa.

"It's your turn for the honor," Heather said with a sigh.

"I'll watch the register. But if you find any Italian Greyhounds, I need to know."

"You know I'm always looking out for the Iggies," Julie said. She leaned over the counter. "Hi, Vesta."

Vesta gave a whine in greeting, her little tail wagging faster, and she scrambled to her feet.

"No jumping," Heather cautioned her, as the tiny dog appeared to be gauging the distance up to the counter. Italian Greyhounds frequently thought they could fly, and she'd already coughed up vet bills for one broken bone when Vesta was a puppy.

Vesta eyed Heather, testing her resolve, and when Heather stared her down, gave a large sigh for her small frame and lay down on the floor to sulk.

Julie hefted the box as the door bells announced a new cluster of customers. "Have fun," she said, winking as she walked away, the skirt of her own elf costume bouncing as she went.

"Hi," Heather called to the party that had just entered. It was a group of middle-aged women who looked overheated and uninterested. Heather wasn't sure if they were looking for something in particular—the shop didn't do much business in July—or if they were just looking for a place more interesting than a grocery store that had air conditioning to pace around in and gossip. "Welcome to the Ornament Shoppe. Let me know if you need any help finding anything!"

They gave her the expected polite murmurs of dismissal and vanished back into the aisles. Heather could hear them complaining about the weather and the traffic and their children.

She was sorting receipts and wondering if the air conditioner in her apartment would be working when she got home when they re-emerged, their conversation having shifted to catty gossip about someone who wasn't with them. One of them had a clearance box of Christmas cards to purchase. Another had found an ornament they wanted and was carrying it carefully in their hands.

"Francine is crazy about unicorns," the woman said, laying it down on the counter after their friend had finished their purchase. "She's going to love this."

Heather completely forgot about the receipts she was sorting, her apartment, the itchy velvet she was wearing, and the small dog lying near her feet.

It was an ornament she hadn't seen before, a blue, blown glass unicorn rearing in a ring of white glass, and she knew beyond a shadow of a doubt that it had to be *hers*.

"I can't sell you that," she blurted.

The customers stared at her.

"I'm sorry," she stammered, scrambling for a reason more coherent than simply *that's mine and you can't have it*. "That…ah…wasn't supposed to go out on display. It's being…it's reserved! I'm so sorry for the mixup! We have a few more unicorns in stock, I think. I can look them up in the computer for you."

The patron, a thin woman with an expensive haircut, looked confused and disgusted. "I wanted this one," she said defensively, and she made a quick motion like she was going to pick the ornament back up.

Heather's blood roared in her ears and her heart pounded as she stepped forward to snatch it away. "You can't have it!"

Unfortunately, she managed to step directly onto Vesta's tail, and the Italian Greyhound gave a yelp of surprise and pain and scurried out from under the counter as Heather, trying to catch herself before her full weight was down on the dog's tail, made a dive for the ornament.

The customer had picked up the gold thread it was hanging on, but Heather had her fingers on the glass, and for a split second, her entire world went away. All she could hear was a ringing battle call, and she was surrounded by pure light and...a compelling presence. Out of the light, there was a draft horse-sized unicorn, white neck arching as he lowered his gleaming golden horn towards her.

Her entire body was on fire, and she was filled with longing.

Julie's voice broke the spell. "What the hell, Heather?"

Heather managed to pry her fingers from the cool glass and the ornament she'd yanked away from the customer fell a scant inch to the counter top. "I don't know," she gasped. The ornament appeared to have survived the drop without damage, but Heather didn't dare pick it up or touch it again.

Vesta was whining at her feet, and the gaggle of customers on the other side of the counter was looking at her like she'd lost her mind.

Which, Heather had to admit, was a distinct possibility.

"I wanted *this* ornament," the client whined.

Julie looked from her to Heather. "It's not for sale," she said firmly. "I'm happy to find you another similar one."

"I don't want another one," the thin woman complained. "I want *this one*. I want to talk to the manager about this."

"I'm the manager," Julie bluffed. "This ornament wasn't supposed to be put out. I'm very sorry to disappoint you. Can I offer you a Christmas in July postcard?"

Barely mollified, the customers took their glossy cards and stomped back out to their cars.

Heather was keenly aware of Julie's concerned gaze but her own eyes kept being drawn back to the ornament on the counter.

"Thanks," Heather said, when she'd finally caught her breath. "I'm not really sure what happened."

Julie reached over her, and before Heather could warn her away, had picked up the ornament. "It's pretty, but I'm not sure what the big deal about it is. I didn't know you were unicorn-crazy."

And nothing happened to her.

Heather waited for the swooning and the flushing, but Julie only frowned at the sparkling glass piece.

"I…I don't know, maybe I had a hallucination or something," Heather said weakly. "I just knew that the ornament was mine, and then I…saw…" She couldn't quite admit that she'd seen a *unicorn*.

"You've been pulling long days," Julie observed with concern. "Did you get heatstroke walking Vesta? Maybe you should head home early."

Heather reached down to where Vesta was trying to get her attention and picked up the wriggling dog. "Sorry about your tail, sweetie," she told the greyhound, who proved her forgiveness with her tongue. "I've been drinking only water, I promise," she told Julie. "But maybe the nonstop Christmas music finally gave me a psychotic break. I think I *will* go home early."

"Don't forget your unicorn," Julie said, and Heather could only stare at it. *Her unicorn.*

"Do you want me to wrap it up for you?" Julie offered after an awkward pause.

"Yeah," Heather said in relief. "Could you?"

Julie wrapped the ornament carefully in tissue paper and tucked it into a box while Heather gathered up Vesta's leash and toys, trying not to be too obvious about her anxiousness while Julie casually handled the fragile ornament and put it into a bag. Heather paid the price on the tag out of her purse.

"Stay cool," Julie called, as she finally left, opening the door out into the sweltering heat.

Heather thought wryly that it was far too late for that.

~

Rez felt the touch of the witch, the seductive caress of her fingers over his glass prison, and his first instinct was to fall into the beauty of her.

The knight's second impulse was to strike out, because there was clearly magic at work here, and magic had betrayed his shieldmates.

He didn't trust either inclination, but he knew, in a dazed way, that everything was *wrong*. He was nowhere and everywhere, floating in a haze of light that lit nothing. There were no limbs to command to kick, human or unicorn, and he was distressingly *powerless*.

It was easiest to concentrate on *her*.

She was not powerless, as was obvious by her effect on Rez. The spell felt subtle, convincing in its gentle persuasion. All he had to do was relax, embrace the promise of her presence, and she would free him...

Which was entirely too good to be true, and Rez had seen too much deceit to believe such absurd fairy tales. It was a *trap*.

He would resist her with the last strength left within him.

Continue the tale in Unicorn of Glass!

SNEAK PREVIEW OF WOLF'S INSTINCT

Writing as Elva Birch...

Don't swear in front of the kids, don't swear in front of the kids, don't swear... Roderick wrenched his shoulder nearly out of the socket trying to reach through the tiny hole under the sink to get to the fitting. Inside his head was a far less censored litany.

"Uck!"

Had he said it out loud after all?

"Uck! Uck!"

Roderick craned his head around and saw a little girl with a blond halo of fuzzy hair standing in the door. She looked about the age of his own daughter, Gabby, but was standing confidently on both feet, a spit-soggy stuffed animal in one hand.

A spry middle-aged woman with salt-and-pepper and electric-blue pigtails swooped in behind her and lifted the child out of the way of the spreading puddle of dirty water leaking from beneath the sink.

"How did you get past the table?" Cherry demanded cheerfully of the child. Her wild-colored hair was at odds with her conservative country plaid shirt and plain jeans. Her feet were in socks, and she was careful to stay clear of the mess.

"Uck!" the toddler replied merrily.

Roderick looked sheepishly at Cherry.

"Yuck," Cherry agreed. "Yuck is right!"

Oh, yuck. Yuck was okay, even if it wasn't at all what Roderick had been thinking.

"What's the news?" Cherry asked, lowering her voice.

"Not good," Roderick said, shaking his head. He'd finally gotten his fingers around the fitting and could unscrew it and draw it out of the tiny access panel in the wet wall. "Whoever plumbed this building ought to be..." he glanced at the little girl chortling in Cherry's arm. "Yuck," he said. "Let's just go with yuck."

He wriggled out from under the sink and inspected the fitting. "I really should take a look at the rest of them, too. If they put these everywhere, you could have a big problem on your hands."

Cherry peered at the fitting. "What's wrong with it?"

"Besides the fact that this is a totally inappropriate fitting for this spot, it's the wrong material. Not to code for potable water."

"Is it toxic?" Cherry asked in horror, exchanging a look with the child in her arms.

"Uck!" the little girl added, trying to squirm free and play in the water on the floor.

"It's relatively harmless," Roderick promised. "But it should all be replaced if this isn't the only one. This stuff tends to wear out faster, especially if it goes through a lot of temperature changes. It also looks like maybe the system was frozen with water in it." He pointed out a crack in the fitting. "There may be other cracks."

"The place was empty last winter," Cherry said,

looking around in despair. "Maybe it wasn't winterized first?"

"I hope you're not having second thoughts about expanding your day care business," Roderick said.

"No," Cherry said firmly, and she gave him a genuine smile. "I'm excited about it. I just dread explaining to Veronica that she's going to have to spend money on the place."

"It's a great place," Roderick agreed.

Cherry's scowl spread effortlessly to an excited grin. "I love it already," she said frankly.

Cherry had been babysitting for Roderick and other shifters in Nickel City for decades, and he'd watched the demand for her services outgrow her house and her ability to watch them all on her own. She'd decided to make the leap to opening a day care downtown and hire a helper or two.

Roderick had been the one to find the place, despite his reservations about the landlord, and was sorry that her opening day had been met with a bathroom flood; he wished that he had better news for her.

The girl in her arms fussed and then seamlessly shifted into a fuzzy little owl chick, beating downy wings in protest of her captivity as she wiggled from her clothes.

"Whoops," Cherry said, easily tossing her in place as she gathered up the clothing. "Clever little Amy, but you still can't play in this mess, even as an owl! I gotta go check on the other kids. My new hire should be here in just a few minutes."

Roderick was surprised by a jangle at the fringes of his wolf's senses. Why would his shifter instinct be excited by *that* news? Sometimes he felt like instinct was a game of hot-and-cold with a kid who had forgotten where they'd hid something, with no hint of logic or direction. He'd learned to treat it with a degree of reserve—since a simple *that way* could lead him right off the edge of a cliff—but never to ignore it.

"Who did you get?" he asked, grabbing the mop to clean up the mess.

"Wendy—you know Wendy from the DMV? Her cousin from Buffalo was looking for work. I haven't even met her yet," Cherry confessed, "but her resume was impressive. She has a certificate in early education, and she worked as a nanny for a shifter family who gave her a glowing recommendation. Wendy said she'd suit me and, well, it's not like I have a lot of choices."

Hiring reliable help for a day care was hard enough. Hiring help for a day care for shifters? That could get complicated. Not only did they have to be part of a secret community, but they still had to meet all the usual human-world qualifications and pass background checks. Maybe his instinct was just confirming that Cherry had picked a good candidate. After all, whoever she was, his daughter would be spending time in her care, so she definitely mattered to his little family of two.

"I'm going to get my ladder and check out the other fittings in the ceiling," Roderick told Cherry. "I'll let you know what I find."

Why would his instinct insist that he was about to find happiness?

*D*iscover *A Day Care for Shifters*! Start with *Wolf's Instinct*!

Printed in Great Britain
by Amazon